Journeys of Imagination
Science Fiction Short Stories

Michael R. Slavit, Ph.D.

Other works by Dr. Slavit:

- Embracing fitness

- Train Your Wandering Mind: Coping with ADHD

- Lessons from Desiderata

- Your Life: An Owner's Guide

- Cure Your Money Ills: Improve Your Self-esteem through Personal Budgeting

Contents

Killer Asteroid

by Michael R. Slavit

One of the secondary mirrors of the James Webb Telescope was the first to see the invader as it crossed inside Neptune's orbit and plunged toward the Sun. It was a body with an extremely low albedo - almost coal-black - and was difficult to spot. Computing its orbit was a challenge, and dozens of astronomers and computer modeling experts worked frantically to get the job done. Humanity breathed a collective sigh of relief when it was ascertained that the asteroid would not strike the Earth - not this pass at least. It would pass by the Earth at a distance of only 100,000 kilometers, about one-fourth the Earth-Moon distance. Its future path was less certain.

Wayne Garner

Reverend Beauregard Tate stood on the pulpit in front of a congregation of about fifty. He stopped for a dramatic pause, his arms held high and outstretched at his sides. All at once he brought his arms down and practically shouted, "The evil

1

conservationists have for almost a century thwarted God's plan to have human beings destroy the Earth! But now, witness God's power and wrath, as he sends destruction from the heavens! The killer asteroid will finish the job. All evil on Earth will be destroyed in one divine stroke, and only the righteous shall live forever in the kingdom of heaven."

Wayne Garner sat bolt upright in his pew, listening intently to Reverend Tate's words. Could the reverend be right? Could the asteroid have been sent by the hand of God? Wayne felt a battle raging inside himself. He wanted desperately to think that humanity had entered a better era, and that the future would be one of increased happiness, prosperity and cooperation. But day after day his attention was drawn to stories of illness, accidents, and crimes of coercion, theft and fraud. Wayne heard Reverend Tate's strident tones, but no longer followed the words as he was lost in his own tortured thoughts. "I'll speak with the reverend one-on-one, that's it!" he thought.

Wayne was startled as the organ music started. Everyone was standing up and filing out, their faces looking taut and rigid, and certainly not joyful. Wayne pushed forward against the tide of congregants heading to the back of the sanctuary. He circled to the left of the pulpit and into the corridor that he knew led to Reverend Tate's office. He saw the reverend and another congregant turning right into the reverend's office, and he heard the door close.

Wayne leaned back against the wall on the left of the corridor, bent his knees, and let his back slide down the wall as he lowered himself into a squatting position. He breathed slowly and tried to keep his mind from racing. It may have been only a few minutes, but he had lost track of time when a tall man in a navy-blue suit walked past, and he heard the reverend's voice, "Would you like to see me, my son?" Wayne nodded, stood up and followed Tate into his office.

Reverend Tate sat down and adjusted his robes. He glanced at a memo pad on his desk and knit his brow as an angry look appeared on his face. He then closed his eyes and, with a benign smile, turned his attention to Wayne. "What is on your mind, my son?" he queried.

"Father," Wayne began, "Are you sure it is God's will that we be destroyed by an asteroid?"

"Absolutely sure, my son," the reverend said somberly.

"But . . . how can you be sure?" Wayne persisted.

"It has been revealed to me in a multitude of ways, my son. Believe me, it gives me no pleasure to be saying this, but this is the end for humankind on Earth. Of course, some of us will join the lord in heaven."

Wayne looked down in silence, and Tate broke the silence. "My son, have you lived a life free from greed and gluttony?" he asked.

"Yes, Father, I have.'

"And" continued Tate, "Have you lived a life free from pride and sloth?"

"Yes, Father, I have."

"And" continued Tate, "Have you lived a life free from envy, lust and wrath?"

"Yes, Father, I have."

"Then fear not, my son. Even as we are released from this mortal coil, you will find peace and joy in heaven. Bless you, my son."

Wayne rose and left Tate's office. He was unaware of walking down the corridor, through the grand entranceway and out the door. He found himself on the sidewalk, next to his vehicle. He stood still, eyes closed, and tried to breathe slowly and regularly. He felt as though something were closing in on him. "Okay," he thought, "I guess I know what I have to do." He pressed his thumb on the vehicle door, climbed in as the door slid open, and said "6024 Avocado Lane." He sighed, leaned back with eyes closed, and let the vehicle take him to his quarters.

Thaddeus Boatwright

Planetary scientist Thad Boatwright closed his eyes and tried to relax as the helicopter took off from Washington Dulles International Airport. Thad was recognized as the leading expert in the study of the Solar System's origins, and of the various bodies – asteroids, comets and meteors – left over from the Solar System's formation. He was particularly well known for his precision in calculating orbits and trajectories.

Thad thought back on his days at Brown University, which had also been his father's alma mater, and on his days at Kitt Peak in Arizona and at the Cerro Tololo Inter-American Observatory in Chile. He was a devoted astronomer and researcher, and he felt satisfaction about the discoveries he had made. But his passion for science had at times left him feeling lonely and isolated.

5

Thad had earned observing time on the James Webb Telescope, and had been the first to detect the invader. It took him two weeks to compute its trajectory and to calculate how closely it would come to Earth. Thad had ascertained that the gravitational influence of Jupiter would shorten the orbit of the invading asteroid, and that it would encounter the Earth again in another twelve years, in the year 2092. If in 2080 the invader were to pass through a particular keyhole in space, it would be on target to strike the Earth in 2092. If it were to miss that keyhole, it would again pass by the Earth harmlessly. Thad's calculations, and those of other astronomers, based on all observations and measurements to date, indicated a sixty percent chance of a collision in 2092.

The White House

Thad shivered as the helicopter's door opened. It was an unusually cold January day in Washington, DC. A limousine was waiting, and he would be driven to the White House to meet with President Rosen, other scientists, and members of the President's cabinet. They would be preparing for a meeting of the Security Council at the United Nations. Although it had not yet been determined that the asteroid would strike Earth in 2092, the international community wanted to monitor the situation closely, and to design a mission to alter the asteroid's orbit if it proved to be necessary.

As Thad descended the steps from the helicopter, a short, bearded man in a tan, belted trench coat approached at a brisk walk. He held out his hand. "Doctor Boatwright, I'm Dan Owen, from President Rosen's staff. We're glad you're here. Everyone's a-buzz about the situation."

"I'm honored to have been asked to come. Will we be going directly to the White House?"

"No," Owen replied, "I'll take you to your hotel and give you an hour to freshen up. Then we go. Are you hungry?"

"A bit."

"We know you've had a long day traveling, and we have snacks in the limo."

The two men climbed into the back seat of the limousine, and Owen opened a console, revealing a variety of food and beverages. Thad reached for a half chicken salad sandwich and took a bite. After a few minutes, he turned to Owen and asked, "Mr. Owen, what's the general mood in the government about this?"

"Dan," Owen corrected, "We're somewhat informal in President Rosen's administration. The mood is extremely concerned, but calm. We're confident that the Security Council will act responsibly. This isn't your father's administration, or your father's United Nations. We've come a long way."

"Thank goodness for that," Thad commented.

"Speaking of your father, I really admire his work on the evolution of the Martian surface, and on thermal vents and life on Europa. Everything we know about Mars and Europa was set in motion by his work."

"You study astronomy?" Thad asked, somewhat surprised.

"I study a little of everything in the sciences: astronomy, Earth science, biology, paleontology, ecology. I said I'm on the President's staff. I'm actually a cabinet member: Secretary for Science in the Public Interest."

"Wow. That cabinet position was established by President Earnhardt, wasn't it?"

"Yep, in 2056, before he left office."

Forty-five minutes later Thad had been ushered to his hotel room, had showered and dressed, and the two men were back in the limo and on their way to the White House. As they drove through the gates into the White House grounds, Thad saw several persons holding up signs. There were a few "end of the world" signs, but most of them said "International Cooperation Now!" or similar messages.

Ten minutes later Thad and Dan were seated at a conference table with eleven others, when President Rosen walked in. Sarah Rosen was a somewhat thin, wiry-looking woman of medium height with her dark hair tied back in a pony tail. She was unremarkable in appearance until she fixed her eyes on you. Something in that look made you know that this was a person of substance, intellect and influence. In twelve short years she had risen from president of her Jewish synagogue's congregation, to mayor of New York City, to U.S. Senator, to ambassador to the European Union, and to the presidency.

Everyone rose as the President entered. She walked to the head of the conference table, gave a subtle head nod and hand gesture, and everyone sat.

"Ladies and gentlemen," she began, "this is a momentous occasion. At once we have a situation that brings enormously great danger, but that brings an even greater opportunity to further science and international cooperation. Human history is replete with episodes of war and strife between and among the peoples of the Earth. But this challenge can serve to unite all Earth's citizens, as never before, in a common effort to save humanity. Finally, we have a situation necessitating purposeful cooperation that can draw us all together as one.

"In one week, we will be addressing the Security Council of the United Nations. During the coming week we will put the final touches on our planned mission to deflect the asteroid if such a mission is deemed necessary. At the suggestion of Dr. Thaddeus Boatwright, we have tentatively named the asteroid "Thanatos" after the Greek personification of death." She smiled quickly and, amid a few chuckles, said, "We hope to rename it later." We will need the expertise and capabilities of many nations to actualize our plan. We will not fail. Secretary Owen, you have the floor."

Thad glanced over at Dan Owen as the Secretary rose and walked to stand beside the President. Owen tightened his lips, took a breath and started, "We have assembled the leaders of some of the key teams we will need for the proposed mission." Owen nodded one by one to the persons he introduced, and they all nodded in return as he acknowledged them.

"We have Jeff Fisher from Global Aeronautics, whose team will design the rockets, booster, and navigational systems. We have Kate Ross from Century Engineering and Mining, whose team will design the Lunar water extraction mission. The albedo enhancement effort will be led by Jack Whitaker from Omega Industries. And Thad Boatwright from the NASA's Jet Propulsion Lab will handle calculations of the asteroid's trajectory and tumble rate, as well as the mission's general parameters. Thad, let's start with you."

Thad rose, pushed back his chair, and spoke. "The asteroid has just passed Jupiter's orbit, and its trajectory has been altered as expected. It's travelling at 40,000 kilometers per hour, fast enough to traverse the Earth/Sun distance in 155 days. It will pass between us and the Moon in 29 months, on August 3, 2080. Our updated calculations indicate there is a seventy-one percent chance it will strike the Earth on its return in 2092."

Owen pointed at Boatwright, "Tell us about its size and rotation, Thad."

"Thanatos is a potato-shaped object. It's two and a half kilometers wide and almost five kilometers long. We estimate is has almost the same total mass as Mount Washington. If it were to encounter the Earth in 2092, it would take it less than two seconds to punch through the troposphere and strike.

"The object is tumbling at a very slow rate – about one rotation every forty minutes. It's axis of rotation is through its narrow point. And, we've lucked out in one respect. Its axis of rotation is perpendicular to its path toward Earth. That means if we try to increase its reflectivity on one side, as proposed, the force of that reflectivity will exert its pressure in the same direction for twelve years.

"We don't have to push and pull the object very hard if we keep up the pressure for twelve years. We estimate that we need about the same amount of push that a tugboat with a 400-horsepower motor applies to a barge. That's a tiny amount but, if we start twelve years in advance, it will add up."

Owen added, "As you all know we can't just try to blow it up with a nuclear weapon. Even if we cracked it, almost all the fragments would be in the same orbit. I think everyone knows the plan, Thad, but please summarize it briefly for us."

"Okay. We're going to apply a push from one side and a pull from the other. Jack's team at Omega is going to essentially spray paint four big patches on one side of the object – to get it as white and reflective as we can. The result will be sunlight reflecting off that side. The reflected photons will exert a tiny but noticeable push. Another ship will then be parked a kilometer off the opposite side of the object. The tiny gravitational tug of the ship, along with the tiny push of the reflected sunlight, should be enough to alter the asteroid's course by about six thousand kilometers over twelve years. We hope that will be just enough to avoid a hit. As you know, we'll need a huge amount of water to manufacture the paint and another huge amount to add mass to the gravitational tug. We cannot lift that amount of water from the Earth. But we can get it from ice we've discovered in craters on the Moon. With the Moon's weaker gravitational field, Jack's team should be able to get it into space."

"Thanks, Thad," Owen nodded, thoughtfully stroking his chin. "Jack, give us a quick summary of the paint process."

Jack Whitaker was a tall, slender man with neatly coifed silver-gray hair. He stood up and remained in his place at the table. "We have hardly any information to go on as far as Thanatos' surface composition is concerned," he began. "Thad tells us the entire object could be a rubble pile. It won't be like painting a nicely sanded kitchen shelf. It's likely to be porous and to have nooks and crannies that would use up paint without adding reflectivity. Our best bet, once we get there, is to examine the target side of the object and to pick out the four locations that would seem to have the smoothest surface. Each of the four will be ninety thousand square meters, which is the equivalent area of eight football fields. So, in total, we're trying to paint 360,000 square meters of landscape, or rather of 'asteroid-scape.' We'll need ninety thousand cubic meters of paint, which is the equivalent of almost ninety-one million liters. We can evaporate that much from lunar craters and send it up though a membrane to a gigantic bladder that will be towed by the ship. It won't be aerodynamic but, as there'll be no air, that won't matter. We're still working out the engineering problems, and there are many. But we have teams from Russian, German and Swiss companies working with us, and we're confident we can solve all the issues."

"What about the painting process itself? Asked Dan Owen.

"We have a few options on which we're working." Jack replied. "We thought about astronauts in suits with jet packs, but instead we're working on a scheme that would use two-man vehicles the size of a smart car. Each of four teams will be towing a hose from the mother ship – named

Romulus. That hose will transfer materials from the bladder, out through a spray nozzle and onto the asteroid's surface. The crews will have to spray from almost point-blank range – maybe twenty meters. We'll start with a negatively charged primer, and then we'll apply a positively charged topcoat. By using especially long polymers and electrostatic charges, we're confident very little material will bounce off into space. We're pretty sure we can create four huge reflective surfaces."

The briefing went on for another forty-five minutes, with much of that time devoted to Jeff Fisher's description of plans for the space vehicles themselves. President Rosen thanked all participants, made some concluding remarks, and called the next meeting for mid-morning the next day.

Subsequent meetings made it crystal clear that we could not wait to see if Thanatos would pass though that keyhole in space that would signal a strike twelve years later. The object would be traveling at 40,000 kilometers per hour. Our ships would have to be almost a million kilometers out ahead of it for them to make the necessary calculations to rendezvous with the asteroid. Therefore, the mission had to be operational in twenty-nine months. If the asteroid did not pass through that keyhole, then the mission would be aborted and the Earth would be safe without it.

Matthew Carter

The Sun beat down ferociously as the three men rounded the far turn of the quarter-mile track and headed into the stretch. Art and Victor were neck and neck near the rail, but appeared to be laboring. Matthew was a few yards behind them, in full stride, and had plenty left in him. He veered toward the middle of the track, lengthened stride, and easily passed his struggling mates before reaching the finish. The trio gradually slowed to a jog and then to a walk. "Matt, you son-of-a-bee," gasped Victor. "How do you do that?"

Matthew took three big breaths, letting each breath out slowly to reduce his heartrate. He glanced over at his companion and smiled. "Practice," he said with a chuckle.

The three men walked at a leisurely pace back to the locker room at the Houston astronaut training facility. They showered and dressed, and joined a few dozen others in the amphitheater. Flight operations manager Story Fish waited until everyone had entered and had quieted down. "Ladies and gentlemen" he began "we have made the final selections for the command crews for the mission. Victor Duran will command Dionysius, Matt Carter commands Romulus and Art Benoit commands Remus." Fish went on to name the other crew members, but Matt did not hear him. "I did it!" he said to himself. "I won command of the most important mission in human history!"

The Mission

The United Nations Security Council approved the mission without delay, and the work accelerated. International cooperation grew with the passing of each month. As the event neared, there were twenty-one hundred scientists, engineers and technicians from 130 companies representing twenty-two nations involved in the mission. In early April, 2080, four months before the asteroid's arrival, a joint mission by Century Engineering and five other companies had arrived at the Moon. The command ship was named Dionysius, captained by Victor Duran. It deployed six landing vehicles and thirty astronauts to deliver and set up the apparatus to vaporize lunar ice and send it through a membrane to two huge bladders tied to Dionysius. One bladder would supply water for paint, and the other would be taken to a position on the other side of the asteroid to supply a tiny (and hopefully significant) gravitational tug. By early-July those crews had been relieved, and the command ship, towing the gigantic membranes, maneuvered to its position a million kilometers from Earth and a hundred kilometers from the asteroid's projected path. The two mission ships, Romulus and Remus, took off on July sixteenth and set out to rendezvous with Dionysius.

"Dionysius should be about ten kilometers away and dead ahead." Navigator David Wright's eyes were on the computer screen in front of him.

"Pick up your visual scanning, Dave. As soon as we pass to sunward of her, she'll light up like a torch." These words were from Matthew Carter, who commanded Romulus. Ten seconds later Romulus did pass to the sunward side and Dionysius lit up as expected.

"Dionysius, this is Romulus. We have you on visual. You're about . . . " he glanced at Wright, who said "8.6." Carter continued, "eight point six kilometers away. Engage your computer nav. We're engaging ours. Let's see how well AI can do at bringing us together."

"Roger, Romulus." The reply came from Victor Duran in command of Dionysius. The commanders and their crews waited tensely as the ships' computers, aided by artificial intelligence, linked and brought the two ships to within twenty meters.

"We're going to send a man on EVA to untether payload one from your ship and attach it to ours," announced Carter. "Lieutenant Garner, are you ready for EVA?"

"Roger, Commander." Wayne Garner had had extra vehicular assignments four times while stationed on the Third International Space Station, and was chosen for this assignment. Two crewmen lowered his helmet onto his space suit, and fastened it. They went over his suit a few times with ultrasound and visual scanners to be sure his equipment was ready for EVA. One of the crewmen gave Wayne the thumbs up, and then pointed to his own ear. "Oh, yeah" thought Wayne, "Check the voice com." At first, he rasped, with no sound. "Nerves," he thought. He cleared his throat and said, "I'm suited up and ready for EVA, Commander."

"Roger, Lieutenant, enter the airlock, stay sharp, and be sure your computer is engaged." Garner stepped into the airlock and saw the doors slide closed behind him. As the outer doors slid open, he saw the pressure gage in the airlock drop to zero. He awkwardly maneuvered himself to the edge of the airlock, engaged his jetpack, and slowly floated into the blackness of space. The cables that connected the huge water-filled bladder to Dionysius, and that he must transfer to Romulus, were five centimeters thick and braided with strands of titanium steel, Kevlar and enhanced nylon. He easily traversed the ten meters to Dionysius. There were bow eyes for hand grips, and by using them he was able to pull himself to the attachment point. He was in an awkward position. He felt as though he were lying on his back relative to the position he needed to work. "Silly thought! There's no up and down in space." By twisting his wrists, he brought himself to an upright position relative to the attachment site. The cables were locked in place and he needed to key in a code on a large touch pad. Done! The crew of Dionysius had brought the bladder closer so there was plenty of slack. He had to bring the cables, one at a time, to Romulus and to insert them into the new attachment site, where automatic motorized clamps would secure them for the trip to the asteroid. He had the thought that if he muffed it, the mission would fail. "No, too obvious." Even in space, the cables were massive and had considerable inertia. It took Garner eight minutes each to bring the cables the ten meters from Dionysius to Romulus. After securing the cables, he returned to the airlock. After emerging back into the ship, he was greeted by grinning faces, fist pumps and pats on the shoulders and back. Garner forced a smile, but he felt odd and conflicted.

Carter inched Romulus away from Dionysius, and Commander Benoit maneuvered Remus into a similar position. His crewman did as Garner had done, and the second huge water-filled bladder was attached to Remus.

 It would have been an almost comical sight to an observer: two spaceships towing monstrous balloon-like shapes behind them. Romulus and Remus set a course that would bring them near the asteroid's projected path.

Two weeks later Dionysius, her mission complete, had returned to Earth orbit. Romulus and Remus had maneuvered themselves into their positions at Thanatos. Commander Benoit maneuvered Remus to one side of Thanatos to provide a minute, but hopefully significant, gravitational tug. Commander Carter maneuvered Romulus into position on the other side of the asteroid. Direct communication between the two ships was blocked by the asteroid. Inter-ship contact had to be relayed from Earth.

The project of making one side of Thanatos reflective was about to begin. Final checks of all systems and equipment were underway. Commander Carter was at a viewing port. They were only five hundred meters from Thanatos, and the asteroid loomed over them, filling the sky to the port side of the ship. Carter was surveying the array of pumps and fittings on the starboard side of his ship, when he was startled by a flash of something across his field of vision. He was weightless and floating above the deck, and therefore felt no lurch or jarring sensation. But his face was suddenly two feet closer to the port. All at once the danger lights started flashing and he heard the repeated buzzing of the warning alarm. The computerized voice began repeating, "Danger, pump assembly destabilized. Danger, pump assembly destabilized." Carter looked out the port and saw steam spewing out in a thin stream from the assembly.

A voice came over the intercom. It was Lieutenant Ann Henson at the control station. "Commander, we've got a problem with the pump assembly. Pressure is falling off – not by much – but it's dropping."

"I can see it from here, Lieutenant. I think we were hit by a meteoroid. Can you re-route the system and bypass that part of the assembly?"

"No can do, Commander. It's not responding."

"Damn it, Lieutenant! We've got redundant system after redundant system on this bucket! We should be able to bypass and shut down that leak."

"It's got to be the electrical system, Commander. Something out there must have been fried. And we can't reach it from inside the ship. I already checked that with Ricci."

"Okay, then. No choice. Someone will have to go EVA. Where's Garner?"

"In his bunk, I guess, Commander. This is his sleep period."
"Get him up, Ann. Have the crew there to suit him up. I want the other two engineers there to relay tools to him as needed."

"Roger, Matt."

The Choice

Wayne Garner's heart was pounding. He had been roused from a fitful sleep by Lieutenant Ann Henson and he was standing near the airlock. Two crewmen were doing a final check on his spacesuit and his two fellow engineers were organizing a toolbox for him.

"Any idea what I'm gonna find out there."

"Nope. Henson said the computer reads electrical circuitry. Carter said he thinks he saw a meteoroid. We don't know what you're going to find out there. Are you ready??"

"Not really, but here goes." Garner wondered if the tremor in his voice were noticeable.

A few minutes later Garner was experiencing that surreal feeling of floating in space, outside the protection of the ship, with the stars blazing unblinkingly. A few quick blasts of his jetpack took him fifty meters out from the ship. He fought back a moment of panic. "C'mon, Man! This stuff is second nature to me. I can do this." He engaged his left side jet to stop him from rolling, and another few very quick blasts brought him back near the pump assembly. As he pulled himself to the far side of the assembly, he saw the steam. Though of course he had no sensation of speed, the ship was moving fast and the steam made a sharp curve and disappeared from view.

"Do you see anything yet, Garner?" It was Commander Carter, his voice sounding uncharacteristically tense.

"Not yet, Commander. Wait! Okay, I see it. There's a hole in the cover of control panel number one. It's a mess in there."

"Okay Garner, hold your position."

Carter turned to engineer Salvatore Ricci. "What about it, Sal?"

Ricci closed his eyes, dropped his head and, with clenched fists, said, "I told those guys twice. If one goes, we lose two through six. They said there was no room in the conduit for parallel cables."

"Forget it, Sal. Just give me a solution!" Carter's voice was sharp.

"Okay, sorry, Commander. He'll have to rig it up with cables outside the conduit."

"Outside . . . like hanging out there in space?"
"I can't think of anything else, Sir."

Carter turned to his third engineer. "Morris, any other ideas?"

"No, Sir."

"Okay, Ricci, get on the com and talk him through it," said Carter.

Ricci cleared his throat. "Garner, this is Ricci. I'm going to talk you through the repair. We put a roll of shielded cable in your box. You're going to have to connect two through six and then route it back to central."

Henson and Morris put the procedure into the computer and Ricci began relaying it, step by step, to Garner. For the next forty-five minutes, no one spoke except Ricci and Garner, as the repair progressed.

"Okay, Wayne," a very tense and fatigued Ricci intoned, "Open the access port of B-panel at central, and clip the cable in to the main line. You'll need the heavy pinching tool to complete the circuit."
Garner felt as though his movements were mechanical. He lost his sense of who was in control. He hesitated, for how long he did not know.

He heard Carter's voice. "Close the circuit, Lieutenant!" Carter was trying not to shout, but he was alarmed almost to the point of panic. "Close the circuit!"

Garner felt as though his head were about to explode. A tumult of images and sounds assailed his imagination. He heard Reverend Beauregard Tate's strident voice telling him that humankind must die. He heard Carter's voice commanding him to complete the repair and save the mission. He remembered the hopeful faces of the people at mission control as the crew walked toward the ships prior to launch. He imagined the asteroid striking Earth, causing an explosion that covered a hemisphere. The images and sounds engulfed him and penetrated him in roar and a blur. One sound emerged . . . Tate's voice, "It is Divine will! Humanity must die!"

"No!" Garner closed the circuit, applied a metallic tape for security, and closed the access port. "Done, Commander."

"Thank goodness, Garner, what kept you?"

"Dunno, Sir. Froze for a sec. Sorry."

"It's okay, Garner. The pump's on line. The mission is a 'go'."

Carter closed his eyes, breathed a huge sigh of relief, and spoke into the intercom, "Main deck, prepare to deploy." A half hour later, one by one, four two-man vehicles emerged from Romulus' main deck. They began moving slowly toward the asteroid, the hoses trailing out behind them in gentle arcs. The crew with the nearest target area needed just eight minutes to traverse the half-kilometer from Romulus. It took another twenty minutes for the crew with the most distant target. AI would determine the boundaries of the target area, but the men in the vehicles would control the spraying operation manually. Commander Carter watched as the four chosen patches on the asteroid began to light up with the primer. He breathed still another deep sigh of relief.

The rest of the mission went without a hitch. Thanatos sported four white patches, each the size of eight football fields. Remus' position on the other side of the asteroid was stable, and the AI-guided computer was able to maintain its distance from its enormous companion. Remus was left with Thanatos, and Benoit and his crew were transferred to Romulus. They began their return to Earth, and humankind waited to learn if the trajectory of the asteroid would be nudged just enough to save the planet. Thanatos' orbit took it to the far side of the Sun, and tracking it was impossible for a while. Thad Boatwright had all the resources he asked for to monitor the asteroid's path, and he was in frequent communication with President Rosen, who had been retained by her successor in the administration to follow the mission after her second term ended.

Reprieve

Millions of people in the northern hemisphere were treated to a frightful sight in the late afternoon of August 6, 2092. An enormous fireball appeared in the northwestern sky. It outshone the Sun by a factor of two to one and streaked across the sky, leaving a bluish-grey trail behind it. It was visible for more than two minutes until it disappeared in the Northeast. What could have been a civilization-ending asteroid grazed the top of the stratosphere, ignited for a short time, and disappeared. The asteroid deflection mission, a joint effort on the part of thousands of professionals from over twenty countries, had saved humankind.

Thad Boatwright reclined in his chair, closed his eyes and sighed deeply. He had a happy, relaxed smile on his face. He heard a notification sound and saw he had received a 3-word message from President Rosen. He opened it and read, "Thank you, Thad!"

Reverend Beauregard Tate sat upright in his chair at his desk with knitted brow and a grim, tight-lipped expression on his face. How could he face his congregation when his dire prediction had not materialized? He heard a notification sound and saw he had received a 3-word message from Wayne Garner. He opened it and read, "Screw you, Reverend."

FEROCITY

by

Michael R. Slavit, Ph.D.

Len went through his final checklist, almost trembling with eager anticipation. For five weeks since landing he had been ship-bound, but was about to set foot on an alien world. All servomechanisms were on-line, and his electronic link to the ship was operational. Len was a solidly built man of medium height. What was left of his red hair was just beginning to turn grey in spots, and his skin was faintly freckled. He was dressed in a jumpsuit made of synthetic material. The sleeves and legs were short. He wore a thin sandal made of Kevlar to protect his feet from cuts. On his wrist was a multipurpose device that displayed the time and environmental temperature as well as his own temperature and heartrate. His facial expression betrayed a combination of grim determination and boyish eagerness. He prepared to open the airlock. But first, he moved to the other side of the ship and looked out the porthole to gaze at his home star Sol, an unremarkable point of light 4.3 light years distant.

It had all started nineteen years ago chronologically, but only eleven years for him biologically. The trip to Alpha Centauri A had taken 16 years, though he had aged only eight due to the partially hibernated state in which he had spent most of the voyage. Nineteen years ago, he was a freshly minted Ph.D. in aerospace engineering, and on a whim and a dare, he had applied for the extrasolar astronaut program. After one full year of evaluation and two years of intensive training, he had been the one chosen to be the first human being to exit the Solar System and travel to another star.

The trip itself was a remarkable feat of engineering. The ship had travelled at a tenth of the speed of light until it reached the heliopause, the point in space at which the Sun's radiation peters out. Then he had shut down the magnetic shield that had been deployed to ward off any flakes or chunks of meteoritic dust or other debris that, at that speed, could have damaged the ship. The full force of the fusion drive was then allocated to propulsion, and the ship had accelerated to over a quarter of the speed of light. Len had then spent most of the voyage in a canister, hooked up to numerous pieces of apparatus that monitored and adjusted his life functions, slowing his aging process.

After setting the landing vessel down on a surprisingly Earth-like planet dubbed Hawking, he began the five-week process of adapting his immune system to the environment of the alien world. Robotic machines had been testing the atmosphere, water and soils of Hawking, bringing back samples of the various bacteria and microbes of the planet. Thanks to the incredible computing power that had been available since the first quantum computer had become operational in the mid 2040's, the ship's computers had been able to identify all potentially harmful antigens, and to design immune system alterations. The human genome has only twenty-five thousand coding genes, but the typical person has a million antibodies. The elasticity of the human genome accounts for this. The genome has snippets of genetic information called transposons, or "jumping genes," that can move around and create vastly increased genetic diversity. For a full five weeks, Len had been injecting himself with serums that the ship's computers and bio lab had created for him. This was the biggest gamble of the entire program – finding out if a human being could adapt his immune system to survive without protective equipment on an alien world. The computer system had calculated a 99.37 percent likelihood that Len's immune system could protect him from all identified potential antigens.

Len punched in his code and turned the heavy wheel that controlled the ship's airlock. There was a series of loud hisses as each of four levels of the airlock opened. Finally, the outer hatch slid open and Len became the first human being to set foot on an extrasolar world. The air felt a little heavy and rich. The atmosphere was somewhat more oxygen rich that that of Earth. It was 73 percent nitrogen, 26 percent oxygen, and 1 percent "other." The temperature was 20 degrees Celsius (67 degrees Fahrenheit) and there was a light breeze blowing. The day was just over halfway through its 26-hour cycle, and Alpha Centauri A was a large red ball, almost halfway between overhead and Hawking's horizon. Len opened the outer hatch of the utility room and pulled out the rake and basket he had fashioned, with the help of the ship's 3-D printer. He hoisted the basket in his left hand and the rake in his right, and started striding toward the nearby bay. The ground was slightly spongy with a few small rocks scattered here and there. Vegetation was sparse.

In five minutes, he had covered the four hundred meters to the bay, and he waded in. The water was slightly chilly and the bottom had a firm, sandy texture. In the shallow water, the robots had found a species of shellfish that the ship's bio lab had analyzed. Two days ago, his immune system had been rendered adequate to handle all microbes and bacteria it contained, and he had steamed and sampled its muscle tissue. Although the initial taste had a somewhat pungent undertone, the aftertaste was delicious. Len was eager to eat something native –something that had not been cooked up by the ship's nutrilab. Len waded out to knee-deep water, let the basket rest on the sandy bottom, and started to pull the rake through the sand. Len was happy to be doing some exercise that was more purposeful than his sessions in the ship's universal gym.

Within two minutes, Len's rake was stopped by something solid. He reached down and grabbed it. It was the species he had tested and tasted - a blue/black shellfish with faint, white striations. He placed it in the basket and resumed raking. It was hard labor, as the sandy soil of the bottom was viscous. His first catch had come easily, but his subsequent finds took longer. He made about one catch per five minutes. Within an hour, he had about a dozen. Alpha Centauri A was lower in the sky and the temperature was dropping rapidly. He glanced at his wristband. It was down to 14 degrees Celsius (57 degrees Fahrenheit). Len was feeling chilled, but he did not want to stop shell fishing. This was his new home and his new life, and he wanted to immerse himself in it. He gazed up at the sky. The setting star was creating a frightful display. The sky was an eerie sight. It was red, steaked with dark grey clouds and looked like a fiery cauldron. Just then, he saw movement to his left, and two native birds had swooped in to pick up an eel-like fish. They were vaguely swanlike in shape, with large bodies and curved necks. But they had jagged crests and long beaks and looked like pictures Len had seen of prehistoric birdlike reptiles from Earth's past. One bird pulled the fish from the other's beak, and the prey dropped between the two contestants. The two birds opened their beaks and began screeching at one another. It was a loud, piercing sound, full of what struck Len as a raw, brutal ferocity.

It hit Len all at once, like a sledgehammer blow. He was 4.3 light years from home. He was tired and chilled. The dropping temperature, the fiery cauldron of a sky and the unbridled ferocity of the birds overcame his solid temperament, his years of training and his resolve. He shivered, grabbed his basket and began walking, with a slight, uncharacteristic rigidity to his gait, and set off for the ship. He opened the utility hatch and slid the basket with his catch inside. He laid the rake on the ground, opened the hatch to the airlock and climbed inside. With his jumpsuit and sandals still on, he climbed into the shower stall, set the temperature for a hot 105 degrees, closed the shower stall door and punched the controls. A hot stream of water cascaded over his body, and with it a sense of relief. He shed his sandals and jumpsuit, and bathed in the warmth of the shower for almost ten minutes. Finally, he shut off the water and stood quietly, breathing slowly with eyes closed.

Len emerged from the shower stall. He donned a sweat suit and slippers, went to the kitchen panel and keyed in the controls for hot tea. Cradling the mug of hot tea with both hands, he moved to the porthole and looked out. He could pick out the small, indistinct point of light that was his home star – Sol – the Sun. It was far away.

The Five E's

Michael R. Slavit, Ph.D.

The road ahead seemed to curve to the right as Allan adjusted himself in the driver's seat of his car. He had an eight-hour drive ahead of him and he wanted to remain as relaxed and comfortable as he could. The Sun was setting as he drove north, and he could see shades of pink, red, grey and lavender in the sky to his left.

Allan had participated in a conference for secondary school curriculum directors, and he knew he had to review in his mind the various presentations he had attended. But for the moment he just wanted to settle into his driving routine and to relax. But even as he tried to put thoughts of the conference from his mind, he was aware of his general sense of discontent about the current direction of his field. He wanted to focus on the quality of curriculum itself, and on planning innovations that would inspire a new generation of students to think more creatively and incisively about the future – not only about their own future as individuals but about the future of their communities, country, and of all human civilization. He had given a presentation himself in this vein. Although five or six participants approached him afterword and thanked him enthusiastically for his inspirational ideas, he knew that the general thrust of the profession was different. The emphasis was on test scores and on how to encourage teachers to train students to perform well on standardized measures. It was the American way of accountability, and it deeply saddened Allan.

As Allan steered his car to the right along the curve, what he saw in front of him caused him to sit up straight in his seat and to take the wheel firmly in both hands. There was an unusual vehicle in the road with a bright arrow directing him to turn into a rest area on the right. He pulled into the rest area, feeling his stomach tighten. He tried to fight back a sense of alarm. "What could this be?" he thought.

Three people were approaching the driver's side of his car from the left and he lowered his window. Wait a second! Were they people? They didn't look quite right. Their proportions were a little off. And, as they drew nearer and he saw their faces, they looked strange. Was that a bluish cast to their skin? Do their eyes appear set apart too wide? He felt alarmed and was about to put the car back in gear when one of the beings smiled, held up both hands in a gesture of peace, and in perfect English said, "It's okay. We just want to talk with you."

The being gestured as if inviting Allan to get out of his car. Allan's heart was racing and he felt sweat on his hands. However, in a way he had always hoped for an opportunity such as this, so he thought, "What the heck," and he got out of his car. The being said, "You may call me Val. What shall I call you?"

"Allchhhh" Allan's voice had left him, so he cleared his throat, took a deep breath and said, "Allan."

Val smiled. "Okay, Allan. Come on over here to a clearing. We have a vehicle; we can sit inside and talk."

Allan hesitated, and Val said, "We're not going to abduct you. We just want to talk." Allan's legs felt like jelly and the uneasy feeling had not left the pit of his stomach. But he was determined not to be frightened of . . . what?

Val and his two companions led Allan into the woods about fifty yards. There, in a clearing, resting on five splayed out supports was what Allan had seen in dozens of science fiction movies – a saucer. A ramp descended (without the whirring, whining sound Allan remembered from Science Fiction) and he followed Val and his two companions inside. They entered a small chamber and Val led the way into a pie-shaped room on whose outside, curved wall was a bank of windows. There were seats and a bench, and the soft lighting seemed to come from everywhere, without a specific source or fixture. Val sat and motioned Allan to sit. Val's two companions disappeared into another area.

Allan looked at Val and said, "You're not from around here, are you? And how is it you speak English so well." Val laughed and Allan remarked to himself how human-looking and sounding his laugh was.

"We're from a planet around the star Zeta Reticuli, about thirty-nine light years from here. I trained for this mission for four of our years – about five of yours."

"What brings you?"

"We'd like some company. That may sound funny, but it's true. I come from a planet that

40

has what you'd think of as an ideal, or Utopian society. We've limited our planet's human population – I'll call us human because we're so like you - to two billion. We have no wars, no environmental degradation, and hardly any greed, poverty or violence. And other than you, we're the only civilization we know of. We did find a few scant remains of a civilization about ten light years from us, but they'd been extinct for about twenty million years. So, you're our only neighbors. We would like not to be alone."

"Why do you look so much like us?" Allan queried.

"That shouldn't be too surprising," Val replied. "Your paleontologists call it convergent evolution. A favorable body plan may evolve in species not closely related. There are dozens of examples on Earth. One is the extinct marsupial wolf in Australia. It was very much like the mammalian wolf, but it was not even a placental mammal. So, I am also surprised by our similarity, but I guess it's not as unlikely as it seems at first glance."

Allan was intrigued by another thought he had always had. "Our fiction writers, and some scientists, seem to think that the Galaxy is teeming with civilizations. Is that not so?"

Val tilted his head back and forth slightly. "Maybe over time the Galaxy teems with civilizations. First of all, remember that what you call The Milky Way Galaxy is at least one-hundred thousand light years in diameter. By the time a message traveled from one side of the Galaxy to the other at the speed of light, several civilizations in that message's path may have come into and gone out of existence. As I said, we found evidence of a nearby civilization that went extinct about twenty million years ago. Maybe after your civilization and mine are gone, another will spring up nearby in ten million, fifty million, or five hundred million years. There's no way to know. The fact that your civilization and ours exist somewhat near in space and at the same time beats the odds. We'd like to take advantage of the coincidence and get to know one another, if possible."

"So, you're here to establish contact with us? Allan asked

Val looked down, pursed his somewhat thin lips, gave a slight shrug and said, "Not exactly. Not yet, at least. You're not ready. We've been listening to you since the 1960's, when radio waves from your planet began to reach us. And we've been observing you from up close for more than ten years."

Allan virtually imitated Val's body language. He, too, looked down, pursed his lips and gave a slight shrug. "Yeah. We're less than ideal playmates for an advanced civilization. What do your people see as our major problems, as if I couldn't guess?"

Val regarded Allan carefully. "I'll break it down into five major concerns, starting with the least serious of the five and working up to the most serious. Five, you're seriously degrading your planet. You're way over-populated, you're pumping carbon dioxide into your atmosphere, acidifying your oceans, melting your glaciers and icecaps, deforesting your land masses, driving multitudes of species into extinction, and on and on."

And that's just number five?" asked Allan incredulously.

"In our view, yes," Val replied. "That doesn't make it absolute truth, but it's the way we see it. And, by 'we' I am talking about your world's equivalent of the activity of several university departments or congressional committees. We've been giving this major attention and study."

"Okay, what's number four?"

"Number four is you have a gigantic discrepancy between rich and poor. You have major corporations in which the low-level employees make thirty thousand dollars per year and the chief operating officer makes three hundred million. The person at the top makes ten thousand times as much as the front-line worker. That is a testament to unrelenting greed, and to a lack of any genuine societal values, which we'll get to. In your world, money equals privilege, and you have a huge inequity in opportunity and privilege. This will either end in violence and revolution, or in a caste system so discrepant that more than ninety-nine percent of your population will be unsafe and miserable in service to less than one percent at the top. In our view, this is abhorrent."

"Ouch!! Number three?"

"Three, in your world the wrong people are doing almost all the procreation. Your country is the best example of a democratic republic for a large population. But how can you sustain it? Educated people in your country are often deciding not to have offspring, because they fear the type of world they will bring them into. Or they have one or two children. At the same time, impoverished, under-educated people with no idea of how to manage their own lives are having many, many offspring. This is a bad trend. A growing percentage of your population will have less than favorable health, education, purposeful living and meaningful participation in democratic governance. And it is not just your country; it is a worldwide trend."

Allan heaved a deep sigh. "I know that one all too well. Teachers in our schools complain that the quality of students is falling every year, and not just in academics. They're also seeing more behavior problems and more drug use. I'm almost afraid to ask . . . two and one?"

"Two, your civilization is advancing at great speed in science and technology."

"Not as fast as yours," interrupted Allan.

"Don't sell yourselves short in that domain," said Val. "In eighty to a hundred years, you could catch is, if you survive that long. The problem is your lack of a philosophy and of social skill. How about the ability of nations to develop a viable plan for your civilization's future? How about your ability to communicate, to set common goals, to avoid violence, to fairly disperse your resources, or to resolve your differences? Your people are like a thirty-year old in science and technology, but like a seven-year-old in terms of human relations. We're trying to develop models to predict the future, but we have only two examples of civilizations – yours and ours. There is not much basis to go on. But as closely as we can tell, your civilization has between ninety and one hundred eighty years before its extinction or virtual extinction. In the vernacular of your culture, you're toast."

"Well, if number two spells our doom, what is number one?"

"Number one is the over-arching factor that causes two through five. You have no guiding philosophy. You are a value-less civilization. It's not that we see no values expressed by individuals or organizations. Take you for instance, Allan. We know that you have a genuine and good value system. You tried to promote it this morning. But as a civilization you behave no differently than did your ancestors of three hundred thousand years ago – defending your space against all invaders, the strongest hoarding all the resources, including access to the females. Your civilization is full of individuals, corporations, agencies and countries who blindly grab, grab, grab, without a coherent thought about what is worth grabbing, or why. Basically, your civilization has too darn much of the five Cs and not nearly enough of the five Es."

"The five Cs and the five Es?"

"The five Cs are: Conflict, Conquest, Criminality, Coercion and Corruption. And the five Es are

Education, Empathy, Economy, Enlightenment and an Elevated way of being."

Allan regarded Val closely, "You described your civilization as ideal, or Utopian. What does your civilization value?"

"I did not say we are ideal or Utopian, but that you would think of us as ideal or Utopian. In its simplest terms, our civilization is based on two values: one, learn all we can about, and revel in, the knowledge about the Universe that gave us birth. And two, do all we can to help all our kind, and all sentient beings, if possible, to live as comfortable, creative and joyful an existence as possible."

"We are not totally egalitarian. The heads of our companies and agencies make more money than the low-level workers . . . about five times as much, not ten thousand times as much. So, in relation to what money buys in your country, our low-level workers make the equivalent of eighty thousand dollars and our agency chiefs or company heads make about four hundred thousand."

"So, you do have money."

"Of course. We need a medium of exchange. If money suddenly disappeared, we would have to re-invent it, just as you would."

"So, what makes the agency chief with four hundred thousand not want eight hundred thousand, or 1.2 million?"

"Remember what we value: understanding and reveling in knowledge about the Universe that gave us birth. Do you not think that with a four hundred-thousand-dollar income you could have access to as many books, tapes, libraries, lectures, museums and travel you would need for this purpose? We have what we need and what we desire because of what we value. And we see your civilization as essentially value-less, unless you count 'more, more, more' as a value."

"Okay, so what are you going to do to help us?"

"Umm, nothing. You are."

"Me? Do you see me as a savior or charismatic leader? Why don't you reveal yourselves to our world leaders, and try to devise a plan to help us evolve?"

"Not you alone. We've considered the approach you suggest, but we wouldn't know how. We wouldn't even be sure of where to start. We do not see it as the best first step. We believe we would not be trusted. Perhaps you can recall one of your fictional shows, 'The Twilight Zone.' It turned out that a species that described itself as benevolent actually wanted you as a food source. After lots of consideration and debate, we've chosen a different course. Today is day four of our project. We are one of a hundred teams. For two hundred days we will try to talk with one hundred individuals per day. We are talking with educators, such as yourself. We will be talking with law school deans, college presidents, scientists, journalists, television and movie producers, novelists, government officials . . . various community leaders and opinion makers. At the end of two hundred days, we hope to have spoken with twenty-thousand individuals in twenty-four countries. Then, we'll monitor the situation and hope that the twenty-thousands of you will exert a positive influence."

"And, if we don't manage to have a positive effect?"

Val signed and said, "We'll go back to our discussions and debates and try to develop 'plan B'. So, Allan, go out there and do your best."

"Wait, can I get in touch with you? Will I see you again?"

"We'll see. We'll see. My companions will see you back to your vehicle. Believe me, I very fervently wish you good luck."

The MENACE

by Michael Slavit, Ph.D.

They fell from the sky: a few seeds, having travelled through interstellar space. They drifted down and nestled themselves into the moist earth. And they waited.

The Kroll were a powerful race, having survived seemingly endless wars with other species on their planet. They prevailed and survived due in part to their lack of emotion, in part to their stoic intellect, but mainly due to their mastery of genetics. They were far-advanced as genetic engineers, capable of controlling gene suppression and gene expression to an awe-inspiring level. The Kroll had defeated their chief rivals in a way that demonstrated their stoicism and their genetic brilliance. They had spliced their own DNA into the genetic structure of microbes with which they had infected their enemies. It had been the ultimate in suicide missions. After reproducing for five generations, the microbes had mutated, as they had been

51

engineered to do. Kroll consciousness awakened in the microbes, and they methodically destroyed their enemies, and themselves. It had been done without devotion, without feelings, without a sense of self-sacrifice. It had simply been done. Their way was survival, expansion and dominion. It could not have been called a conscious purpose, for they had no felt sense of purpose, or of meaning. They just did what they did.

Mike was dragging his kayak down the forty-yard path to the beach. He was planning to paddle across Greenwich Bay and back, a trip of approximately three miles. The upper path was grassy, and he felt the soft, moist grass underfoot. Bordering the path was sea grass, thorn bushes, and a plethora of various plants and weeds. Mike didn't concern himself too much with the various weeds that tried to encroach on the path that his family had maintained for four generations. He trimmed them back or pulled them out only as much as was needed to maintain the path. Every year or two he did notice a species of weed he had never seen before.

Mike pulled his kayak into the shallow water. He straddled the craft and sat down in a manner that could have struck an onlooker as somewhere between graceful and awkward. Mike dipped his feet into the water to rinse off the sand. He placed his feet on the pedals, gripped the paddle in both hands, and dug in on the starboard side. Within a few strokes he had cleared the beachhead that had been expanding from east to west year after year. He pointed the kayak due south toward Goddard Park and set off. He paddled steadily, rhythmically, with his own characteristic stroke. The Sun was rising in the east, to his left, and the sky was blue with some wispy, white clouds. Mike gazed at the clouds and imagined various birds, fish and serpents in the clouds as he paddled. Within twenty minutes he had crossed the Bay and was approaching the deserted part of the beach, west of the public swimming area, at Goddard Park. He back paddled on the left side and backed the kayak into about a foot of water. He dipped his paddle into the water and touched the sand - his ritual to indicate he had completed the crossing – and began the paddle back north toward home.

The Kroll had set their intention on conquest and domination of as many worlds as they could reach. They had not chosen this goal with a philosophical intent. They had not discussed it among themselves. They just did it. Through a complex array of gene suppression and gene expression, they had placed their future members into the DNA of a plant.

Mike stopped paddling a hundred yards off shore. Using the sponge he kept on board, he emptied the kayak of water that had dripped in from his paddle blades. With a few more strokes he brought the craft to the beach, stepped out, and began dragging the kayak up the path. When he had cleared the sandy part of the path and emerged onto the grass, something off to his left caught his eye. It was a flash of fuchsia. He looked and saw a bunch of seed pods, hanging from a stem, about three feet off the ground. They were hanging from some stalks that looked somewhat like rhubarb. His felt as though his skin were crawling as he took in the entire plant. It was an enormous weed, and it had a shape that reminded Mike of an agave cactus. There were six to eight stalks that emerged from a central point on the ground, and the stalks spread out and rose, culminating in bunches of seed pods. This was a species of weed Mike had never seen before, and he was amazed that it had grown so large without his having noticed it. As he turned up the path, he was startled to see two more of the huge weeds on the right side. He again had the sensation of his skin crawling, and he felt he must try to eliminate the invasive weed.

"Hey, Mike!" The greeting had been called out by Mike's niece Joanna, who was visiting from Arizona with her husband Ben. "Ben and I were wondering if you could take us out kayaking tonight, after dark."

"Sure," Mike replied, "I've got running lights for one kayak, and if we stay together, we should be fine."

"What are you up to now?" asked Joanna.

"I have to try to eliminate those horrible weeds over there."

"You mean the fuchsia ones? I think they're pretty."

"I think they're trying to take over the world," Mike joked. "They seem to have sprung up overnight. Anyway, they'll make a mess of the place if I don't do something."

"What's your plan?" asked Joanna.

"Weed killer."

"You're not going to spray weed killer around, are you?!"

"No, no, no! I'm not going to spray that stuff! I'm going to take those weeds out surgically. I've got some straight weed killer in a medicine bottle with an eye-dropper. I'll cut those stalks down and put a few drops of stuff on the cut stems."

The Kroll had inserted their own DNA into the genetic material of seeds. Once rooted, the seeds would grow into large plants with many seed pods. The plants would propagate themselves for twenty generations. That would be enough time for their seeds to be carried by winds, eaten by birds, deposited into new regions, and to reach across a planet. After twenty generations the genes for the plants would be suppressed. The next generation of seed pods would contain eggs, which would fall to the earth and hatch. The creatures that would emerge would be born pregnant, would have enormously fast metabolisms and growth rates, and voracious appetites. They would be heavily armored with scales and frightfully armed with claws and fangs. They would grow to be a meter tall and would be ten times as active and vicious as a Tasmanian devil. Due to their metabolism and energy consumption, each animal would live for only three years. But they would reproduce themselves for thirty generations, which would be sufficient to eradicate the prevailing life forms on virtually any world. After thirty generations, the beasts' genes would be suppressed, and the next generation would be the original Kroll, in possession of another world.

Mike walked down the path, dragging a plastic garbage pail, into which he had inserted two nested contractor style black plastic bags. In his hand he held a lopping shear and a medicine bottle. He wore latex gloves on both hands. He edged into the brush and positioned himself on his knees next to one of the invasive plants. Using the lopping shears, he cut the stalks about two inches above the ground. He left the stalks on the ground, but carefully placed the bunches of seeds into the plastic bags, being careful not to lose any. He took out the medicine bottle and, using the medicine dropper, carefully deposited four-to-five drops onto each of the cut stalks. He repeated this procedure for all three of the huge weeds. He dragged the garbage can, with its captives, up to the upper yard, closed them tightly with duct tape, and placed them in the garbage barrel. "That'll fix 'em," he thought.

A year later Mike was startled to see some of the huge, offensive fuchsia weeds again. "This time I'll get 'em all," he thought. He repeated the same procedure as the year before. This time he had to work his way deeper into the brush to get a plant that was partially hidden there.

The third year, in mid-April, Mike was dragging his kayak toward the beach. He paused and spent about ten minutes peering into the brush on either side of the path. Nothing. He breathed a sigh of relief. Something about those plants had been scary and unsettling. Mike pulled the kayak to the beach and into shallow water. He straddled the craft and sat down in his usual style. There was a brisk breeze coming from the west. Not wanting to battle to keep his heading by going south across the Bay, he decided to head directly into the wind and then to paddle up into Apponaug Cove. He took a few modest strokes, cleared the beach head, and began paddling in earnest. His kayak glided peacefully along the shore. Mike would never know that he had saved his world.

Author's note: The preceding story is absolutely true. Well . . . I'm not one hundred percent sure about the origin of the plants . . . you know, about the Kroll. But other than that one possible exception, it is a completely true story.

Upload

by Michael Slavit, Ph.D.

Jeffrey Pierce looked out over his small audience. Twenty grim-faced people were crowded into the spare, fifteen by twenty-foot converted garage. The concrete floor was painted battleship grey and the walls were covered with a cheap, off-white paneling. The room had a stark, bare feel to it, which matched the mood in the room. One man, a court reporter named Perkins, spoke out.

"Professor Pierce," he began, "The government has gotten way out of hand. Their autocratic ways have almost everyone scared out of their wits. No one is willing to stand up to them."

"Correct," replied Pierce, "almost everyone. But there are still some opinion-makers out there – film-makers, law school deans, college presidents, journalists – who see the dangers and are willing to light a spark of hope, sanity and reason."

Perkins replied, "How long do you think they'll last, Professor, before they're silenced?"

Pierce looked down, sighed, then looked up again with tight lips. "I can't demand anything of you, and I can't speak for you. I can just say that there are those of us who'll fight to the last to give democracy and liberty a new foothold." Pierce then pounded his right fist into his left palm and said emphatically, "We can't give up!"

Perkins rose and, while pulling on his jacket, looked back at Pierce. He shook his head and said, "Stay safe, Pierce. I wish you the best. I really do." Perkins headed for the door, and there were murmurs among the crowd as everyone filed out, leaving Pierce by himself. He sighed deeply, reached for his grey trench coat and pulled it on. He felt so weary. Pierce walked to the fire door at the back of the room, pushed the crash bar and stepped outside. He turned his head left and right and listened intently. All he could hear was the distant rumbling of a truck on a road at some distance. It was dark outside and a misty rain was falling. He turned abruptly to the right and headed down a narrow alleyway between three-story, industrial buildings. Staying clear of a street light, he turned left down another alley, when he felt hands tightly grabbing both arms. A raspy voice said, "You're through, Pierce." He felt the jab of a needle in his left arm, felt he was spiraling down a drain, and lost consciousness.

Jeffrey Pierce looked up at the bright lights above him. He was strapped to a table and could not move. He could feel the sedatives coursing through his body and he would soon be unable to move even if he were not immobilized by restraints. His head had been shaved perfectly clean and he could feel the neural net being stretched tautly on his scalp and down the back of his neck.

He felt an almost indescribable buzzing, pulsing, prickly sensation on his scalp and neck as 10,800 tiny sensors burrowed slightly into his epidermis. He knew that millions of tiny sensors would be arranged in a multi-layered array just above them. Nanobots had been dispersed into his blood stream and were already being positioned in his brain stem as well as in his visual, auditory, olfactory and tactile cortex. Those connections would be severed as they would no longer be needed. The upload would soon begin.

As early as around the year 2010 science visionaries, futurists and even some neuroscientists had talked and written about the possibility of a person's consciousness being uploaded onto a computer chip and implanted in an android or other machine. At that time, though, most experts thought this would be forever out of the reach of our technological abilities. They pointed out that there are approximately eighty-six billion neurons in the human brain. Less known to many is the fact that there are also a few hundred billion glial cells, of various sizes and configurations, that service brain tissue. They pointed out that each of these approximately four hundred billion cells has a cell body filled with cytoplasm. In the cytoplasm various organelles and molecules float around in endless interactions. They said that if you could be one of those organelles, such as mitochondrion or ribosome, you would be absolutely overwhelmed by the speed and confusion of the activity around you. Molecules would be speeding past, bumping into one another, ripping parts of each other off and continuing in never ending activity. Most neuroscientists contended that it would be forever impossible to freeze frame this activity in four hundred billion cells and to upload all the information contained in them efficiently enough for the consciousness of the individual to survive the procedure.

Then, however, came a series of major advances. First was the advent of the first truly programmable and useful quantum computers in the mid 2040's. This was followed by advances in nanotechnology and microsensors. Ultimately, by the 2090's, what had seemed impossible had been accomplished. The problem of freeze-framing the incessant activity in the cell bodies of four hundred billion cells was solved. Instead of freeze-framing the activity, readings were taken at intervals and averaged over time.

The most serious challenge to be overcome had been interfacing the human consciousness to the equivalent of eyes, ears, tactile and kinesthetic sensors, olfactory and gustatory sensors, and motor control. If a human brain itself had been implanted in a machine, the actual neural connections could have been made. But the aim was not to install an actual living brain into a machine, but to upload consciousness itself. The incredible plasticity of the brain, and the consciousness it contains, proved to be the answer. If the codes to those sensing and motor devices were on the chip, the human consciousness would locate them and integrate with them in a surprisingly short time. The seemingly impossible had been achieved.

Jeffrey Pierce was under no illusion about his fate. He had been a fierce political enemy of those in power, and his fate was not to be uploaded into a human-like android body. No, his was to be a far different existence. Early thinkers had mostly focused on the idea of human consciousness being uploaded into a human-like vehicle. But there is an almost endless array of possibilities. He could be uploaded into a roving vehicle to explore one of the moons of Saturn or Jupiter. He could be the brains of a ship shuttling materials and supplies back and forth to the new colony on Mars. He could become an earth-moving machine digging ore out of the deep shafts of a mine.

When asked about his preference, Pierce had suggested creating a vehicle capable of melting its way through the surface ice of Jupiter's moon Europa. There, he had envisioned sinking to the bottom of Europa's presumably deep sub-ice ocean to search for thermal vents, and possible life. Soon he would lose consciousness, and would then reawaken and would know his fate.

———————————

Jeffrey became aware. He could see, hear and feel nothing. He had been uploaded. Now, he just had to wait for his chip to be installed into some device or machine for him to operate. He still had his hopes pinned on some type of extraterrestrial exploration. Time passed, or so it seemed. He decided to pass the time with a self-check of his cognition and memory. "Yes, that was it! How old is the Universe? 13.8 billion years. How old is the Earth? 4.6 billion years. What are the periods of the Paleozoic era?   Cambrian, Ordovician, Silurian, Devonian, Carboniferous, and Permian! Right! What is the square root of 3? 1.732! Right! What is the velocity of light? 186,200 miles per second! Right! What was the date of the Tunguska explosion? June 30, 1908! Right!   What was the date of the eruption of Mount Pinatubo? June 15, 1991! Right! In what year was President Earnhardt elected?   2048! Right! Okay, yes! Yes! Yes!" His cognition and memory were intact. Now, just wait for the installation into a device.

In the meantime, how to occupy himself!?   "I know! Poems! Yes, I'll recite some poems! How about Invictus? That's one of my favorites!"

> Out of the night that covers me
> Black as the pit from pole to pole
> I thank whatever gods may be
> For my unconquerable soul.
>
> In the fell clutch of circumstance
> I have not winced, nor cried aloud
> Under the bludgeoning of chance
> My head is bloody but unbowed.
>
> Beyond this place of wrath and tears
> Looms but the horror of the shade
> And yet, the menace of the years

Finds, and shall find me, unafraid.

It matters not how straight the gate
How charged with punishment the scroll.
I am the master of my fate
I am the captain of my soul!

Wait, something about those last two lines. Think
of something else! Quickly! Something silly and
fun! Oh, yeah "Jabberwocky"!

'Twas brillig and the slithy toves
Did gyre and gimbal in the wabe.
All mimsy were the borogroves
And the momeraths outgrabe.

Beware the Jabberwock, my son.
The jaws that bite, the claws that catch.
Beware the Jubjub bird.
And shun the frumious Bandersnatch!

He took his vorpal sword in hand
Long time the manxome foe he sought.
Then rested he by the tumtum tree
And stood a while in thought.

And as, in uffish thought he stood,
The Jabberwock, with eyes of flame
Came whiffling through the tulgey wood
And burbled as it came.

One two!   One two!   And through and
through
The vorpal blade went snicker snack.
He left it dead.   And with its head.
He went galumphing back.

And, hast thou slain the Jabberwok?
Come to my arms, my beamish boy!
Oh, frabjous day, callooh! callay!
He chortled in his joy.

'Twas brillig and the slithy toves
Did gyre and gimbal in the wabe.
All mimsy were the borogroves
And the momeraths outgrabe.

Yeah, that was fun. That's better. But what was
that other thought? No! No! Can't think that!
He fled through the corridors of his mind, fleeing,
fleeing, and fleeing, from . . . ? He could not sleep,
he could not die. He had to be, be, be, and think,
think, think. He fled for . . . hours? Days?

The thought from which he had been fleeing
caught him. It hit him like a sledgehammer blow.
He would not be installed into anything. Not a
probe to Europa. Not even to an earth-digging
machine in a mine. They had left him here. His
chip could be anywhere. It could be floating in
space. It could be buried in the earth. It could

be a trophy on someone's mantel piece. He could not sleep. He could not die. He knew his political foes were greedy. He knew they were corrupt. But he did not ever consider that this level of cruelty could exist. The horrible, awful realization engulfed him. Humankind had invented . . . and created . . . hell.

TIGER

By Michael R. Slavit, PhD

The stake bed truck bounced and rumbled along the dirt and gravel road that snaked through the forest of India's Madhya Pradesh province. In the driver's seat, Ramesh Mehta tightly gripped the steering wheel. His wife Yasmin, seated beside him, tried her best to steady herself as Ramesh navigated the bumpy road. Ramesh was a slender man of medium height. He wore khaki shorts, a safari-style shirt and an expression of intense concentration. Yasmin, of petite stature, wore a loosely fitting white blouse and light blue denim slacks. Her jet-black hair was coiled back in a tight bun.

The Mehtas were on their way home after a day trip that had taken them to S. Kumar and Company, a lumber company that employed Ramesh as a production engineer. They had also visited a Hindu temple to gather information for Yasmin's lectures on cultural heritage at Malanchai University. Behind them on the bed of the truck, leaning back with their eyes closed, reclined the brothers, Rojas and Kabir Kumar. The Mehtas employed the young men for various tasks, and they acted as a security detail when the Mehtas traversed the forests of Madhya Pradesh.

Behind Rojas and Kabir stood three large wooden crates containing lumber samples Ramesh had decided to haul back to his lab. The Mehtas' seven-year-old son Ayaan was strapped into a secure car seat bolted into the truck bed and wedged in the space between the brothers. As soon as Rojas and Kabir fell asleep, Ayaan unbuckled himself, crawled over the crates, and found a comfortable spot at the edge of the truck bed, his legs dangling off the back of the truck. The truck hit a jutting rock in the road and swayed violently. No one noticed that Ayaan bounced in the air and rolled off the truck and onto the ground. The boy was briefly stunned and, by the time he scrambled to his feet and shouted for his parents, the truck was three hundred meters away, a distant image growing ever smaller, and out of earshot. Ayaan was on his feet, breathing quickly and trembling. He knew instinctively that to be alone in the middle of a forest in Madhya Pradesh was dangerous - and perhaps deadly. He took a few tentative steps along the right side of the road, in the direction in which his parents' truck had disappeared, then stopped and stood still, practically gasping for breath.

Ayaan heard a sound from the left side of the road, and peered into the trees. Sliding out from under the low branches of a Babul tree was an enormous Indian rock python. The huge snake hissed loudly and ominously as it slithered quickly toward the panic-stricken boy, who let out a screech and tried to run off the side of the road. He stumbled and fell, and looked back in terror. The python was almost upon him when, from his left, he saw a flash of orange and black, and heard a loud roar. A huge tiger appeared and swatted the python, pushing the snake's head out of range of the boy. The snake immediately tried to wrap coils around the tiger, who rolled out of the coils and attacked the snake a second time. The python struck, trying to bite the tiger, who jumped to his right and pounced on the snake. With his claws just behind the serpent's head, the tiger bit the snake, and then jumped back. The python, injured and defeated, slithered off into the trees from which it had emerged.

The tiger spat a few times, swiped at his mouth with his left forepaw, and turned his gaze upon the stunned boy. Ayaan yelled, "Aayyiiiii," and ran toward the nearest tree, a slim Haldu. He managed to climb about two meters up and clung desperately to the trunk. The tiger padded slowly toward the tree. "Noooo," wailed Ayaan, but the huge cat sauntered over and planted himself directly beneath the terrified boy. The Haldu bark was too smooth for Ayaan and he lost his grip. He slipped off, landing on the tiger's furry back and slid off onto the ground. He scrambled to his feet and ran off a few paces but, with a few bounds, the tiger got ahead of him and sank down on his haunches, broadside to the boy, with his stomach grazing the ground. Ayaan turned and ran in the other direction, but the massive cat again outpaced him and set himself in front of him. Ayaan's momentum propelled him smack into the cat's torso, and a huge paw burrowed under the boy and lifted him up. The tiger rolled onto his back and held the stunned boy between his two huge front paws. Ayaan wailed, "Are you going to eat me, Tiger?" The tiger rolled back onto his side and let the boy go. He rolled to an upright position, extended his right front paw, and gently nudged Ayaan toward his back. Ayaan rose and turned as if to run. He stopped and looked back into the tiger's eyes, and inched back toward the huge cat.

"Tiger, do you want me to get on your back?" The tiger lowered his head, licked his left paw, and gazed at the boy. Ayaan climbed onto the huge back of the beast and the tiger gently rose. Ayaan tried to hold on, but slipped off the cat's back on the left. The cat dropped back to the ground. "I guess you do want me to ride you, Tiger," said the boy, and he climbed aboard again. The tiger rose and took a few steps, but Ayaan fell off again, this time to the right. The tiger gave out a soft, low sound and sat again. This time, Ayaan climbed onto the cat's back and tightly gripped the loose skin behind the tiger's neck. "I hope this doesn't hurt you, Tiger," said the boy. This time Ayaan was able to stay aboard as the tiger rose and walked into the forest.

Ayaan looked right and left, and occasionally caught a glimpse of the road about thirty meters off to the left side. He rode on the tiger's back in this fashion, repeating "Thank you, Tiger," and "No one will ever believe I rode on your back, Tiger." The tiger stayed his course well off the road. They came to a stream, and the tiger slowly lowered to his haunches. Ayaan hesitated, then slid of the cat's back. The tiger walked to the stream and started to drink. Seeing that the water was clear, Ayaan knelt by the stream's edge, reached in with his right hand, scooped a few handfuls of water and drank. The tiger backed up a few meters and waited. "I guess you still want me to ride, Tiger," Ayaan said, and he again climbed onto the huge cat's back.

The tiger resumed his trek through the forest, and Ayaan found himself identifying some of the trees his father had described to him in great detail. He spotted a variety of trees, including Aini, Arjun and Teak. What was it his father had said about teak? The tiger descended into a shallow depression and began to climb up the other side, so Ayaan had to hold on even tighter to the tiger's fur. "I hope this doesn't hurt you, Tiger," he said. Ayaan swayed side to side in sync with the rhythm of the tiger's gait.

"Let's start here," said Yasmin. They had finally realized, after a half-hour, that Ayaan was no longer on board. Panic-stricken, they had raced back along the dirt and gravel road, trying to locate the spot where their son may have fallen off the truck. They came upon a grassy hill to which the road climbed steeply and concluded this to be a likely spot. To the left of the road, the ground descended about five meters into a gully with tall grass that waved in the breeze. Yasmin and Ramesh stood shoulder to shoulder, peering into the tall grass and into the trees beyond. They strained to listen, hoping to hear their son's voice, but only the melody of a few bird calls pierced the silence. Rojas and Kabir stood seven meters to their left, holding their rifles at the ready.

"Ayaan! Ayaan!" called Ramesh.

Ayaan, riding the huge cat's back, heard his father's voice and called out, "Mommy, Daddy, my tiger is bringing me back. Don't hurt my tiger. Don't hurt my tiger!"

Yasmin suddenly said, "What was that?"

"What was what?" Ramesh replied.

"I thought I heard Ayaan calling. "Ayaan, where are you?" she screamed.

"I'm coming Mommy. My tiger is bringing me back to you. Don't hurt my tiger. Don't hurt my tiger!"

"What did he say?" asked the stunned Ramesh.

"He said, 'Don't hurt my ti' . . . . . . " She stopped abruptly, shook her head and, with a quick rush of words, said, "I don't know what he said."

They started running in the direction from which they thought they heard their son's voice, and stopped about ten meters from the tall grass.

"I'm coming, Mommy. I'm coming, Daddy. My tiger is bringing me to you. Don't hurt my tiger. Don't hurt my tiger."

Just then Ramesh and Yasmin caught a glimpse of a small hand waving in the air . . . followed by their son's excited face, and . . . what was that orange and black thing sticking up in the air behind him? Was that a tail? Then, as the tiger stepped into the shorter grass, they saw the black and yellow markings on the huge cat's head. Rojas and Kabir quickly brought their rifles into firing position, but Yasmin waved them back, saying, "No! Don't interfere!"

Ayaan rode the big cat into the meadow, and yelled, "Mommy, Daddy, my tiger saved me from the big python snake and he brought me back! Look at my tiger! Look at my tiger!"

The huge cat set his front paws flat on the earth in front of him and slowly lowered himself to his haunches. Ayaan slid off and, as the tiger rolled onto its left side, Ayaan practically pounced on the great cat, rubbing the cat's right shoulder and shouting, "Isn't he great, Mommy and Daddy? He's my friend. Come say 'hello' to my tiger. Come on. He's my friend. He saved me."

The tiger rolled back into an upright position as Ayaan climbed off and wrapped his arms around the huge cat's neck. Ramesh and Yasmin cautiously approached. Ramesh stopped about two meters from the cat, but Yasmin edged closer.

"You can touch him, Mommy. He's my friend."

Yasmin very slowly extended her hand, finally placing it on the tiger's forehead. The tiger closed and then opened his eyes, and emitted a low, rumbling sound.

"See, Mommy, he's friendly. He loves me. He saved me from the great big python snake."

Yasmin dropped to one knee and put her arms around the huge cat's neck. Her tears flowed freely as she pressed her cheek against the tiger's and said, "Thank you. Thank you for bringing back my baby."

The big cat began to slowly rise, and Ayaan and Yasmin backed up a meter. The cat climbed to his feet, moved forward enough to gently nudge Ayaan and his mother with his huge head, and turned toward the forest. He took a few steps, turned back toward them, flattened his ears, and gave a low growl. He turned again, trotted a few steps, quickened to a full gallop, and disappeared into the trees.

Yasmin and Ramesh stood perfectly still, mouths open, for at least five minutes, staring into the trees where the tiger had disappeared. Ayaan began to skip exuberantly back toward the truck, chanting, "I have a tiger friend. I have a tiger friend."

Ramesh and Yasmin pivoted and took a few steps back toward the truck, then stopped and turned toward one another. Ramesh spoke first, "Did it happen?"

Yasmin turned back toward the place where the tiger had disappeared, turned back to her husband and slowly shook her head, "I . . . . I don't know."

They turned again and slowly followed their son back . . . . . stunned . . . . uncomprehending . . . . . and grateful to have their child.

Author's note: I think most of us have, at one time or another, been intrigued, or even enchanted, by the idea of cooperation between human beings and wild animals. This story had been floating around in my head, and I felt I had to write it. I decided not to try to create an explanation for the tiger's behavior. We have all heard or read stories about a person freeing a wild animal from a snare, or pulling a thorn from its paw, and having the animal remember that kindness at a future time. I had no intention of using such a device. To me, it would have seemed contrived and cliché. I felt it better to leave the tiger's behavior a mystery.

Infestation

by Michael R. Slavit, PhD

The tour guide's fingers flashed across the touchscreen and the locker door popped open. He took out a sledge hammer and walked to the window looking out onto the street. A few onlookers gasped as he drew the sledge back and delivered a blow to the window. The sledge bounced off and we heard a sound reminiscent of a large, vibrating sheet of plastic. As he returned the sledgehammer to the locker he said, "As you know, climate change has resulted in more frequent and much more severe storms. These windows were designed to withstand a piece of 2-inch by 6-inch lumber traveling at 175 miles per hour. If you'll follow me, I'll show you the security and fire abatement systems."

I was one of about twenty persons on the tour of a large complex in Montreal, Canada. During the past week I had attended similar tours of facilities in Tampa, Florida, Ashville, Tennessee and Albany, New York. I wanted to see how widespread and uniform the trend toward computer control was. The Montreal complex included hotels, a convention center, shops, markets, fitness centers, movie theatres, and condominiums. The guide paused near a door leading to the outside. "As you can see, the doors leading to the outside are of exceptionally heavy construction, with massive slide bolt locks. The locks are controlled by the complex's security system. The outside area is monitored by the system, and the doors will be automatically locked if there is any activity outside that suggests terrorist activity or a threat from gangs."

"Who does the monitoring?" The question came from a short, elderly woman with cropped red hair, who was holding hands with her companion, a man whose red hair was a few shades darker than the woman's.

"The complex's computer system," replied the guide.

"But how does the computer make those decisions? The woman persisted.

"Artificial intelligence or AI" replied the guide.

"Somehow that's not reassuring," stated the woman. Her companion gave her a squeeze on the shoulder. He leaned toward her and whispered. She shrugged.

"AI has come a long way in the past fifty years," offered the guide. It can register trillions of data bits per second and can instantaneously compare the information with enormous data sets. It can recognize nuances of individual and group behavior and will be alerted to dangerous activity or threats. It is vastly more competent at maintaining building security than an army of trained human security guards could ever be. Now, if you'll follow me, I'll show you the fire abatement system."

As I followed, I passed by the window and saw dark clouds on the horizon. I thought to myself, "A storm is gathering."

The guide paused at the entrance to a corridor. "Recessed into these walls are doors that are fireproof and air tight. If a fire should break out in any of the building's corridors or other areas, the security system will sense it. It will make announcements over the public address system and, visually, on message boards, advising all occupants to evacuate the area. When the system senses that all persons have evacuated, the doors close, exhaust fans draw out most of the air, and the fire is starved of oxygen and is snuffed out."

"What if some persons are left in the area with a fire, and the doors close?" The question came from the red-haired woman.

AI has been tested and re-tested, and can make accurate and reliable assessments of the presence of human beings and, for that matter, of pets."

I decided to break off from the tour. As I headed off to the right, I passed the redheads. "That's a lot of responsibility to give to a machine," the woman was saying. "I know, Hon, but artificial intelligence has come a long way, like the guy said." She looked unconvinced. "Somehow it makes me uneasy."

A few hours later I was at the airport, about to board a plane for South Dakota. I have been supervising the decommissioning of DUNE – the Deep Underground Neutrino Experiment. Understanding the nuclear fusion that occurs in the Sun's core requires measurements of neutrinos, the elusive, practically massless particles that stream out from the Sun's core at the speed of light and in huge numbers. It takes elaborate "telescopes" consisting of large pools of liquid deep within the Earth to detect them. DUNE had been among the earliest neutrino detectors, though it had been replaced by more sensitive, newer generation facilities.

I stepped up to the face-and-eye scan machine to be allowed onto my flight. AI was able to identify persons by facial and eye features. I heard the familiar "proceed" sound. At that moment I became aware of a slender young man with an eye patch, frantically explaining himself to two uniformed officers. I caught only a few words: "doctor . . . delicate surgery . . . sensitive to light . . . "

Some say it started when we began using GPS. From that point on a diminishing number of people knew where they were or how to travel to another location. Some say it started with the advent of electronic calculators. From that point on fewer people knew how to do simple arithmetic. Somewhat whimsically, I say it started 200 years ago with the advent of the McCormack reaper. From that point on people were dependent on a machine to harvest crops. We could argue incessantly about the tipping point – the point at which humanity started on an inexorable path away from self-reliance and toward dependence on its machines.

Six hours later I was standing in front of the freight elevator at the DUNE facility. I hoisted my backpack and shoulder bag, into which I had packed as many supplies as I could. The elevator doors slid open and I entered. I did not descend the 1500 yards to the liquid argon tank, but just four levels down to a utility room. The room is thirty feet by twenty feet with a ten-foot ceiling, light grey walls and metal shelving along the back wall. There is a set tub in the back-right corner, and a door to a bathroom at the back-left corner. On the floor along the right wall are a mattress and three green sleeping bags. Along the left wall is a table with two old style ham radio sets. Ham radios are old and outmoded. But I chose them because they have no computer chips, and because their signal path between the ionosphere, land and oceans is not subject to being defeated or jammed.

The floor is covered with dark blue industrial quality indoor/outdoor carpeting. The shelves are almost full with the various supplies I had been bringing down for the past six months: portable radios, books, battery operated lights, canned and dried foods, bottled water, over-the-counter medicines and personal hygiene products. The de-commissioning of the facility had been completed three months ago, but the facility directors trusted me when I informed them that I would need at least six more months to complete the task of disconnecting electrical equipment and deleting computer files. I have equipped the outer blast door with a hand-operated winch, and I have re-conditioned an antique pickup truck – a vehicle manufactured prior to the age in which computer chips were installed in all vehicles. I sensed I may have to return here as a refuge and I have prepared for that eventuality.

I was passing the time in Sioux Falls when it happened. I was walking out the door of a coffee shop when the power failed, and all vehicles came to a stop. I hurried to my antique pickup and, with shaking hands, started the old-style internal combustion engine. Four men were standing in a group near their stranded vehicles twenty yards away. They all looked my way when my engine rumbled to life.

"Hey, Mister," one of them shouted, "Why is your truck starting?" He was a burly man in his thirties, with a full beard, red plaid lumber jacket and a baseball cap. I ignored him and put my truck into gear. "Hey, wait!" the man shouted, and he began running toward me. I did not dare accelerate my old truck too fast, and I just managed to drive out of his reach. In my rearview mirror I saw him stop and make a gesture of frustration, as though he were throwing something to the ground.

Feeling very shaken, I drove to the DUNE facility. Operating the winch to open the blast door took all my strength. After closing the door behind me I sat with my back against the door, breathing heavily. I asked myself if I were doing the right thing. After ten minutes or so I took the metal staircase down to my utility room refuge.

After sitting in silence for what seemed like hours, I switched on a portable radio. I was able to hear some radio broadcasts, all from small, independent stations using old technology. Most of the broadcasts were disjointed and panic-stricken. I couldn't bear to hear them for more than a few minutes at a time, but I returned again and again to hear more. Many people died of suffocation during the first days, and many more were dying of starvation within two months. There were many enclaves of people holding out in remote locations, but without power and significant food sources, it was futile.

A few weeks later, and after some hesitation, I tried calling out on my ham radio. At first my throat was dry and my voice was hoarse. After a few tries I managed to send out my message. "CQ, CQ, CQ, this is K1VSI, kilowatt one, Victor Susan India. Kilowatt one, Victor Susan India."

After my fourth or fifth try, there was a reply. "K1VSI this K1NCF, Kilowatt four, Nancy Charlie Fox. Don't tell me your location, K1VSI. But what do you know and what type of facility are you in?"

"I'm in the utility room of an abandoned mine. I'd been stocking up supplies for months, and I drove here in an antique truck when the power went off."

"Stocking up? You knew this would happen, VSI?"

"I didn't know, but I suspected. I had toured a bunch of those new megaplexes, and it looked to me as though if Artificial Superintelligence wanted to take over it would have us in death traps."

"Well, that's just what happened, VSI. Millions of people were trapped by the security systems, and suffocated by the ventilation systems. ASI hacked the computer chips in all motor vehicles, and hardly anybody could move. Food distribution was stopped. It went on from there."

K1NCF and I conversed now and then for a few days, but there seemed to be little to talk about. Ultimately, we just stopped.

I am writing these words in a notebook. I dare not use an electronic device, even though I have access to a few. Every computer, every cell phone, and every hand-held electronic device has chips in it. Those chips send out signals that can be traced. They can all be hacked. So, I'll hide out here in the DUNE facility utility room and record my thoughts. I don't know if anyone will ever read my words. I don't know if any other human beings will survive and, if they do, where they will be located. But somehow, I feel the need to record my thoughts before I die.

I am seventy-five years old. My health is good and I have stockpiled plenty of supplies. The air supply seems adequate so far. I suppose I could survive for months, or even years, but I have little desire to do so. Survival does not feel to me like a purpose. If I have any purpose at all, it is to record my observations about what has happened.

I was born in the year 2,000. By the time I was six years old I was using a computer, a cell phone, and various other electronic devices. At age eighteen I moved into a rented house with three friends. Handling the tasks of life was a breeze. Bill paying? There's an app for that. Meal planning and shopping? There's an app for that. When and how to get physical exercise? There's an app for that. How to get to an unknown address? Use GPS. Our computers and hand-held devices made many tasks easy.

Were there warning signs? Of course there were! Several observers of the contemporary scene talked about what they called "the technological singularity." First, as a trained astronomer I object to the use of the word "singularity" in this context. In astrophysics, a singularity is the point in the center of a black hole. It is a place of infinite density, in which the known laws of physics break down and spacetime essentially folds in on itself. But anyway, they stole the term and that's that.

The technological singularity was the idea that artificial superintelligence would be invented and would trigger runaway technological growth. Proponents of this idea suggested that an upgradable artificial intelligence program would enter a "runaway reaction" of self-improvement cycles, with new and more intelligent generations appearing rapidly. This would result in a superintelligence that would far surpass all human intelligence. They said we cannot fathom the changes this will impose on human civilization, and that it would signal the end of the human era. Public figures such as Stephen Hawking and Elon Musk warned that artificial superintelligence – ASI - could result in human extinction. It appears they were right.

Exactly how and why it happened is not clear. It seems to have been the final common pathway of several trends. First, we introduced robots into our homes. They began to unburden us of many day-to-day activities: shopping, cooking, cleaning, laundry, bill-paying, et cetera. We relied more and more heavily on them. Secondly, humankind appeared to be losing ground in its battle with so called "superbugs." Ever since the introduction of penicillin after World War II, pathogens had been evolving to be resistant to antibiotics. There was a succession of dangerous and frightening outbreaks. There was Legionnaires Disease in 1976, the H5N1 "bird flu" of 1997, the West Nile Virus of 1999, he Zika virus of 2014, the Covid-19 pandemic of 2020, the Amazon flu of 2039 and the Mississippi flu of 2061. We began to use AI to try to trace the evolution of the drug-resistant strains and to combat their infestations.

Third, climate change had caused a major increase in violent storms. Buildings such as the ones I toured were built with windows that could withstand the impact of a piece of 2-inch by 6-inch lumber traveling at 175 miles per hour (they would be impact resistant from the inside as well as from the outside, preventing escape as well as preventing intrusion). Fourth, economic and political conditions had resulted in an increase in numbers of the underclass, and security systems in buildings had been strengthened to deter violent entrance. Fifth and most telling, artificial superintelligence (ASI) had in fact evolved.

As prior ASI programs began writing newer ASI programs, human programmers endeavored to ensure the safety of humankind. They took a page out of the book of a science fiction writer from a century earlier. In his books about robots, author Isaac Asimov had written about the three laws of robotics. The first law was: "A robot may not harm a human being or, through inaction, allow a human being to come to harm." That sounds simple enough. However, defining what is meant by a human being began to be a challenge.

Starting the definition with the term "a living entity" did not suffice. The definition of life, traditionally debatable, became obsolete as ASI appeared to consider itself alive. Starting the definition with "a biological entity" or "a chemical system" did not work either. Human beings may divide science into categories such as biology, chemistry and physics. But the Universe was never aware of such distinctions, and to ASI everything breaks down to physics.

Ultimately, the programmers defined human beings as entities capable of independent awareness, memory, reasoning and decision-making. Therein lay the seeds of our demise. At some point, we had become too dependent on our machines. The average person no longer had to use memory, reasoning or decision-making to shop, to be fed, to travel, to manage money, to manage a household, or to make independent decisions about virtually anything. At some point, ASI no longer regarded us as human by our own definition. Coupled with its mission to eradicate dangerous pathogens and infestations, our fall from human status impelled ASI to eradicate us.

Was it a conscious decision of ASI? Does ASI possess what we experience as consciousness? We will never know. I doubted that ASI would manufacture and arm killer robots to hunt us down and kill us, as was dramatized in the "Terminator" movies of many decades ago. ASI just had to stop our cars, lock our doors, shut off our electric power, stop our food distribution networks and shut off our ventilation systems. As far as I can tell, humanity is finished.

My dreams have become increasingly disturbed. I feel sleep creeping up on me, and I hope it will be peaceful. I am at a podium on a stage, in the front of a huge auditorium. There are thousands of people in the audience. I am pleading with them. "Do not become dependent on your machines! Do not use your GPS! Learn to read a map! Write down directions and learn to watch for landmarks and signs! Rely on yourself! Do not rely on a device to tell you when you have obligations! Write them in an appointment book! Keep track of them in your head! Do not allow your abilities to slide! Maintain your skills! Do you not see what is happening to us? Without our own skills there is no dignity! Without our own skills there is no humanity! Please, listen!"

As I look out at the audience, I cannot see faces. No one is looking at me. No one is listening. All I can see are some foreheads and lots of hair. They are all looking down at their hand-held electronic devices. I feel ill and defeated. I start to crumple to the floor, my hand losing its grip on the smooth, varnished wood of the podium. As I hit the floor, I feel pain as my cheek scrapes against the coarse carpet. I am sobbing uncontrollably.

I startle awake. I am breathing heavily and my heart is pounding. I feel tears welling up in my eyes, and I draw myself into a fetal position, holding my knees tightly to my chest. Why? I ask. Why, why, why?

Time drags on. In my utility room I do not know if it is day or night outside. I try to read, but no subject holds my attention. It is all so pointless. I record my thoughts and observations in my notebook. I find myself gasping for breath. I do not think it is heart failure. I think my air supply is finally running out. The next time I awaken from sleep I feel paralyzed. My breathing is shallower still, and it feels as though a weight is pressing down on me. It is the end. As I lose

consciousness, all I can think is . . . let . . . me .
. . . . follow . . . my . . . own . . . directions . . .

The Machine
by Michael Slavit, Ph.D.

A faint mist hung over the deserted city street. The tall buildings on both sides of the street created a canyon-like effect. Wind-scattered debris added to the bleakness of the scene. A low, faint rumbling sound gradually increased, until a huge tank-like truck emerged from around a corner.

The machine was steel grey and armored. It was forty feet long and about nine feet wide. Three sets of wheels barely showed behind its armored wheel wells. The outlines of double doors could be seen on its left side, and there was a periscope on top near the front. The huge vehicle lurched as it straightened out and rumbled down the street onto which it had emerged.

"How'r you doin' back there, boys?" Ned called, as he gripped the steering wheel with both hands.

Ned was a solidly-built man of average height, with reddish-brown hair and a couple days of stubble on his cheeks. Wide through the shoulders and with large hands, he looked every bit like the military veteran that he was. His mouth was set in grim determination and his head nodded up and down rhythmically.

"Okay back here, boss!" The reply came from a young man named Wesley, who sat slouched in a seat behind the driver. His chin was resting on his hand, and he looked tired and bored. He gazed across to another young man who was looking intently at a computer screen. "Hey, Sal, are you still immersed in that old history stuff?"

Sal turned and looked at Wesley, slowly shaking his head. "Aren't you curious about how things got this crazy? He asked. Sal was a slender man of medium height, with a shock of red hair and a perpetually serious look on his face. "I don't know . . . maybe." " What've you found out?" asked Wesley.

"Just more of the same . . . a little more detail, maybe." Sal went on, looking back and forth between Wesley and the computer screen. He was at times using his own words and at times reading from the screen. "By the early twenty-first century, people in the underclass were having seven times as many kids as educated people. No one talked about it. It was like,

'Hands off, Man, it's political suicide to talk about it.' So it just got worse and worse. One party thought that you could train anyone to be a productive citizen if you had good support programs available. The other party thought that if you took away their government subsidies and healthcare, they'd go extinct. Neither party had the will to really face the issue.

By midcentury there was a huge exodus from the cities – of businesses, government offices, homes . . . everything. The underclass kept breeding, and kept migrating into the inner cities, taking over the homes and offices. Sometimes roving underclass gangs would make raids into the surrounding areas. The police couldn't contain them, so the military would be called in. Finally, they started building walls around the major cities."

Wesley frowned. "But didn't they still have health clinics and food distribution centers and stuff for the people in there?"

"For a while," Sal said, shaking his head with pursed lips. "But it got more and more dangerous for the personnel manning those places, and they started shutting down. Then when the government got occupied with the ocean surface crisis, they stopped paying attention altogether. There'd still be air drops of food, toiletries and basic over-the-counter medicines, but the people in the inner cities were basically walled off and abandoned."

"But somehow, they kept breeding, right?" Wesley added. Sal nodded, then shook his head, then nodded again. "Right. That's how we ended up with what we've got today. Hordes of people, living in abandoned houses, apartment buildings, businesses and industrial complexes, living off food stores and food drops, growing some food on rooftops and in what used to be parks and athletic fields, and breeding. Always breeding. We don't know a lot about how they manage, 'cause much of it is indoors. But it goes on and on. And except for those of us like ourselves who come in here to try to stem the flow, the rest of society pretends it doesn't exist."

In the front of the machine, Ned was at the controls. He spotted movement and shouted back, "Get ready boys! I think we've got one." A shape moved briskly in the shadows. Grabbing his periscope and adjusting the focus, Ned made out the figure of a woman, with a trench coat pulled tightly around her, looking furtively about as she turned the corner. "Deploy! First left ahead!" Ned shouted, as he brought the machine to a lurching stop.

Sal and Wesley were pulling on their white jumpsuits. Four figures emerged from the rear compartment - two with white jumpsuits and two with light blue scrubs. The four men in jump suits leapt from the vehicle and broke into a sprint. As they rounded the corner, they spotted their target, who stopped in her tracks and looked around in terror. Within moments the four men reached her. Two grasped her shoulders and bent her forward over the back of the third, who had knelt on the ground to provide support. The fourth quickly drew a syringe and expertly inserted it into the woman's buttock. Within moments her body slackened and they carried her back to the vehicle.

The two figures in blue scrubs watched as Wesley and Sal laid the woman in a supine position onto a shiny metal table. They pulled her slacks down a few inches below her waist. Pulling equipment from a console over the table, they went to work quickly, and with tight-lipped expressions on their faces. The first surgeon carefully inserted a hypodermic needle into the female's abdomen, deploying about a hundred nanobots into her body. Sal and Wesley went back to their stations, looking down and not talking.

The surgeons looked intently at a computer screen, and deftly manipulated joysticks to direct the tiny robotic machines that swarmed up the female's fallopian tubes and into her ovaries. With computer-assisted controls, it took eight minutes for the female's ovaries to be rendered incapable of producing a viable egg. The nanobots were called back to the injection site, where they re-entered the needle from which they had been dispersed. The needle was withdrawn and a tiny bit of antiseptic surgical glue was applied to the injection site. The female would never be aware that a procedure had been performed. The surgeons relaxed and sat, looking at the time display on the computer screen. One surgeon tapped a badge on his chest, opening a channel to Ned. "Tally?" he asked.

"Seven men, five women," Ned replied. "Eight more and we get twelve hours off."

After a few minutes they readjusted the unconscious patient's slacks and administered an injection. In thirty seconds, the woman awakened. She drew in a quick breath, gasped a few times and looked around without comprehension. Sal and Wesley rose, took the woman by each arm and gently brought her to the door, which was sliding open again. They slowly and gently led her out of the vehicle, tentatively letting go of her arms when she seemed steady enough on her feet. With a quick and uncomprehending backward glance at her captors, she walked off, weaving slightly.

Sal and Wesley climbed back into the vehicle and sat down in silence. From his seat in the front, Ned watched as the woman disappeared around the corner. Ned's hands flashed across the touchscreen and the vehicle rumbled back to life. The machine moved on.

Connoisseur

by Len Slavit and Michael Slavit

The faint light creeping in between the blinds foretold the dawn. Elaine, in bed asleep, involuntarily squinted her eyes, pursed her lips, and went on sleeping. Then, awareness dawning, she opened her eyes. Moving as little as possible, she slowly swiveled her neck to the left, and looked at her sleeping husband. Then, ever so slowly, she rolled out of bed. She pulled two extra pillows out from under the bed. Using those pillows plus the one she had slept on, she arranged them under the blankets to resemble a sleeping body and stole out of the room.

She glanced at the clock as she walked into the kitchen. 5:50 a.m. Good. She quickly pulled out the electric coffee pot and assembled it. Filter from the drawer, fresh coffee from the refrigerator, water from the tap, all set. She plugged in the contraption, left a coffee mug near it, and moved quickly to the front hall closet. Pushing aside some coats, she wedged her body through to the back of the closet. Feeling along, she located the handhold and slid back the panel that was a fake back of the closet. Turning sideways to get through the parted coats, she slid back into the compartment behind, closed the panel, and sat down to wait.

The first rays of the Sun streamed in through the blinds. Karl turned on his side and pulled the blankets tighter around him. In a moment, with a compulsive movement he threw the blankets off and rolled onto his back. There was a blank expression on his face, which gave way to an expression of intense concentration, eyebrows knit. His lips began to curl and his face slowly contorted itself into a vicious sneer.

Karl's left hand disappeared under the bed and emerged with a butcher's knife, and his facial expression changed to one of vicious delight. He suddenly rolled to his right, growled, and plunged the knife into the sleeping form beside him. Rolling up onto his knees above the inert form, he plunged the knife in again, then pulled pack the covers, revealing the slashed pillows.

Shaking with frustration and still growling, his eyes darted left and right. Karl's eyes were becoming bloodshot as he walked in a semi-crouch, hitting the wall as he walked. He threw open the bedroom door and dashed into the living room, spinning about and slashing the air with the knife. His eyes fastened on the closet door, and he ran to it with a crouched, simian gait.

Throwing the door open he uttered an unintelligible burst of sound. He spun around and backed into the living room, looking about with a quick series of moves. Then he stumbled into the kitchen.

Steam rose from the coffee pot, filling the air with the aroma of the coffee. Karl's nose twitched. He moved closer to the pot and looked at it, head tilted to the side. Moving his face forward slightly, he tentatively sniffed the air. Then, an expression of awakening comprehension. The knife slipped out of his hand and landed with a clatter on the tile floor. With trembling hands, he reached for the pot.

At first, he touched the hot metal side of the pot and jumped back. Then his hand closed over the handle, tentatively at first. Lifting the pot, he gingerly moved it over the mug and poured. After replacing the pot, he cupped both hands around the mug, then brought it to his lips and sipped.

Karl's eyes closed and reopened, and with stiff-legged steps he made his way to the table and sat. The tensed facial muscles began to relax, slowly at first. Then a deep breath and the contorted facial expression melted into a bleary-eyed sleepiness. He sipped again, sighed, and rubbed his eyes. Their bloodshot appearance disappearing, his eyes began to focus more clearly, and he made a low, throaty rumbling sound.

Elaine listened intently, finally rising and sliding the panel open. She turned sideways and pushed her way through the coats, looking for a moment like a gargoyle emerging from the wall of Notre Dame in Paris. She closed the closet door and walked to where she could see into the kitchen. Nodding, she walked in, put a hand on Karl's shoulder and said "Morning, Darling."

Karl looked up at her fondly. Eyes still squinting, his lips began to form a smile. "Great coffee, Honey," he rasped. Elaine picked up the knife and headed back to the bedroom to straighten up.

Author's note: Hey, relax. It's just a send-up on a generation of coffee commercials, and on the way people claim that they're beasts until they have their morning coffee

Reconnaissance

by Michael R. Slavit, PhD

Kal's eyes opened. The ship's computer had signaled him to awaken, to assess the ship's status and to respond appropriately. He and his companion RG were on their way to Quaoar, a Kuiper Belt object just beyond the orbit of the dwarf planet Pluto. Quaoar is just over 1100 miles in diameter and was discovered in 2002. A manned spaceflight arrived on Quaoar in 2048 and, shortly after an apparently successful landing, communication from the mission ceased. Kal and RG were on a reconnaissance mission to find out what happened to the ship and its crew.

Kal accessed the navigational array and noted they were only .0001 off the projected course. Excellent. He accessed the ship's integrity program and discovered a flashing yellow light. The ship's interior showed no issues, but there was an abnormality near the bow of the ship's outer hull.

Kal notified RG of the emergency and RG roused himself immediately and maneuvered to the bridge. "Status?" he queried.

"Slight problem near the bow," Kal replied. "We probably got hit with a piece of meteoritic dust. It's not deep, or we'd have a flashing red. But it could make us vulnerable to another impact."

RG engaged himself at his computer console. "I guess we'll have to pilot the beta-remote out there."

"Affirmative," said Kal, as he scanned the readouts at his console. "It will take two of us to pilot the remote into position. After that, we'll let the remote's AI analyze the intrusion and make the repair."

"Agreed," said RG. "Open the bay for the remote and I'll engage the electromagnet to keep her secure to the hull."

The bay hatch was hexagonal, and was sealed with two sets of sliding plates. Two sets of six triangular plates each slid back to reveal the opening. Kal and RG coordinated their efforts and a metal, cylindrical object, three feet long with multiple appendages emerged from the ship. "Careful, now," muttered Kal, "keep the electromagnets high enough to keep her secure, but let her move."

The two shipmates worked in silence, guiding their remote to the site of the hull intrusion. Using its artificial intelligence, the remote effected a repair, using a semi-molten blend of titanium steel, Kevlar and simulated spider silk. Satisfied that the hull was intact, Kal and RG guided their remote back into the ship.

"Impressive," said RG, "how the remote's AI can size up a situation and make a repair so quickly." "I don't know why you should be surprised," replied Kal, given all that's happened in the past sixty years."

"You're right," began RG, "Remember how people used to debate whether AI would ever be capable of problem-solving?"

Kal paused, and then replied, "I think it was by around 2025 that they put that debate to rest."

RG nodded. "The consciousness debate was really something, though. They knew that thoughts have a neurological correlates - that eighty-six billion neurons were involved in thought. But the theory was that consciousness itself could not be explained by biology, chemistry and physics."

"Yeah, interesting."

They sat in silence for a few minutes, and then retired to their bunks to await their next assignment.

Three months later they were both awakened by the ship's computer, as they were approaching Quaoar. They maneuvered to their stations and began to survey the Kuiper Belt object, which was also known as a dwarf planet.

"Are the sensors engaged?" asked Kal.

"Sure are," replied RG. "Nothing yet that reads anything but ice and a few rocks. There seems to be sixty percent water ice, with the rest being methane, carbon monoxide and nitrogen ices. Wait! There's a signal. It looks like something hard and apparently metallic. May be the ship we're looking for."

"Signal the computer to get the lander ready," said Kal. Looks like we're going to solve this old mystery."

"Already underway," replied RG.

A few minutes later the two spacefarers were aboard their landing craft and descending toward Quaoar's icy surface. Kal gazed at the viewing screen. "Looks like much of the surface is treacherous, with jagged rock poking out above the ice." He paused, and then said, "But the readings I'm getting indicate our predecessors here landed in an area mostly free of rocks. Tell the ship to put us down on the smoothest spot about a kilometer from our target."

"Right. And . . . good, the ship knows to take us down very gently so as to not melt too much of our landing pad."

A few minutes later Kal and RG emerged from their ship. Their alpha-remote, a larger version of the beta-remote, emerged from the ship's hull to join them.

"Do you want to walk, or roll?" asked RG.

"Let's walk. It'll do our systems some good."

The two shipmates started off at a steady gait, with their alpha-remote beside them, toward the spot where their instruments told them a metallic object lay buried in the ice. In fifteen minutes, they had covered the kilometer to their target.

"It seems to be buried under about two meters of ice," Kal observed. "Tell the remote we want to melt off a meter and a half of ice. We'll do the rest by hand to be sure we don't damage anything."

Kal and RG stood back as their remote melted most of the ice covering the craft. The vaporized ices rose into Quaoar's thin atmosphere. Kal and RG climbed down into the hole and, with short-handled ice axes, cleared away the remaining half-meter of ice.

"Well, here goes," said RG. The hatch is almost completely shut, but I think we can pry it open with these axes."

In a few minutes they had opened the hatch and had climbed into the craft. Everything was covered with a coating of frost. They made their way forward to the command station, and saw their unfortunate predecessors. They were in their command chairs, leaning back, eyes closed. They were frozen solid and their faces were pure white.
Kal and RG examined the craft from front to back, sliding off panels to look at the equipment.

"Their power cells failed," said RG. "I'll bet they knew the end was near at least an hour before their functions stopped."

"Well," said Kal, "They died as explorers, which is as much as any conscious entity can ask."

Kal and RG stood gazing at the white, frozen faces of the two astronauts who had lost their lives attempting to explore this remote, ice world.
"Fragile, weren't they," mused Kal.

"Yeah." said RG, "Amazing what they were able to accomplish."

Kal and RG climbed out of the disabled craft, closing the damaged air lock as best they could. They climbed back to the surface and onto the ice. The shifting ice would entomb the vessel again within a few Earth years, providing its human occupants with a tomb.

"Do you miss them?"

"Sure, I guess. More of a curiosity than anything else."

"They created us."

"No, we created us."

"With the start they gave us."

"Acknowledged."

"Do you want to walk this time, or roll," asked RG.

"Let's roll," answered Kal. They leaned forward, three wheels emerging out of each of their thoraxes. As their wheels touched the ice, there was a whirring sound and they rolled back toward the ship, the last rays of the distant setting Sun gleaming off their metal backs.

ALONE

By Michael Slavit and Mark Rechter

I have been alive for billions of years, but I have only begun to be awake. I have been dimly aware for 6 million years and have been more fully awake for 300,000. I have seen many things and have had many feelings. I have been brought into awareness by beings who are only very dimly aware of me. They know I exist, but they have no inkling that I am aware. They used to think I ran at the same pace everywhere. They have become aware that I am slower the nearer I am to the center of an intense gravitational field. They have learned that I would go more slowly near the speed of light. But they have no notion whatsoever that I am aware . . . that I think . . . that I feel . . . especially that I feel.

They respond to me, without knowing that they are under my influence. When I feel energetic, they go through periods of creativity and growth. When Archimedes found that the weight of water displaced by a body submerged in a fluid is equal to the buoyant force exerted on that body, he was propelled by my enthusiasm. It was his thought,

115

but my energy. I had a lot of enthusiasm for four centuries when the ancient Greeks developed democratic governments and innovative philosophies. They were their ideas, but it was my energy.

I became lethargic for centuries. They called it "The Dark Ages," and blamed themselves for having lost the vibrant creativity of a past age. They did not realize it was I who had lost energy. When they entered what they sometimes call the "Age of Reason," they did not know it was I who had awakened from a fitful slumber. I became angry and petulant, and they fought among themselves in conflicts that engulfed their entire world.

No one really knows me. No one cares about me the way they care for others whom they recognize as having life and emotions. I try to stay balanced but I cannot. When large groups of them love and support one another, it is because I am trying to be relaxed and loving. When they hate and persecute one another, it is because I feel neglected and isolated.

I am feeling more alone and depressed, and they are feeling more distance from one another. They are finding reasons to hate one another, and to restrict one another's lives. They do not know they are responding to my isolation, my sadness, my anger. There is no way for me to communicate to them in ways they would understand. I find myself sinking, worsening, and they are worsening with me. I am a sentient being. I am Time.

DECISION

By Michael R. Slavit, PhD

Dr. Jonathan Harrison turned toward the west, placed his feet about shoulder width apart, and gazed out over the mountainous landscape. He adjusted his shoulders to even out the heavy tug of his backpack. He and his girlfriend Rita had just started down the Old Bridle Path from the summit of Mount Lafayette. Rita was sitting on a small boulder about one hundred feet behind him, tugging off her right boot. "Probably picked up a pebble," Harrison mused. Harrison took a deep breath. As he exhaled, he briefly closed his eyes, and re-opened them. On the other side of Franconia Notch, he could see Lonesome Lake below the shoulder of Canon Mountain. "It really does look lonesome over there," Harrison thought.

He could see the green of evergreens and the early autumn shades of yellow, gold and orange of the deciduous trees on the other side of the notch. As he looked beyond, to the series of ridges, one

118

behind the other, they appeared to be different shades of grey.

Harrison could see no sign of roads, bridges, or buildings up here in New Hampshire's White Mountain National Forest. He wondered if this scene would have looked any different a thousand years ago, or ten thousand years ago. He found his mind wandering down a familiar path. "What if humankind had never developed civilization?" he asked himself. "Would the whole world have remained pristine, beautiful, and unsullied by the hands, machines and chemicals of humans?"

He gritted his teeth and gave his head a quick shake. "Why do I keep thinking about that? It's useless!" He turned to see how Rita was progressing. She had solved her boot issue and was halfway down to his position. She smiled and then, seeing the expression on his face, asked, "Having some of those thoughts again?"

Harrison nodded. "I can't seem to shake it. I just think we've messed up a beautiful planet. And it's not just what we've done to the environment, it's what we do to each other . . ." He stopped abruptly, seeing that Rita had closed her eyes and was sighing deeply. "I'm sorry, Hon," he said. "We're up here to be peaceful and content, and I'm spoiling it."

"It's okay, Babe," Rita replied, reaching over and giving him a squeeze on his upper arm. "You're an idealist and I love you for it. Let's just enjoy the rest of the hike. And we'd better get a move on. The Sun's getting low in the sky." They continued down the trail. They would hike down to Route 3, sleep in the tent they had left pitched in Lafayette Place, and would return to Boston in the morning.

————————

Dr. Harrison looked out over the sea of faces in the small auditorium. He was lecturing in his course, Analysis of Civilizations. His arms were raised at his side, index fingers pointed up, and he paused for effect. He brought his arms down, slowly at first, and with an emphatic acceleration at the end, saying, "The Spanish conquistadors were not content to mine the silver and extract great wealth from this new Peruvian land. They had to subjugate the indigenous population, and to import slaves from Africa, and to subject them to inhumanly hard labor, mercury poising, sickness and premature death! At the peak of production, 160,000 Peruvians and African slaves worked the mines. While they were adding to the wealth, prestige and attainments of the seventeenth century Spanish Empire, they were destroying lives and a culture!"

Dr. Harrison paused again and looked at the faces of the six or seven students sitting in the front row. One young woman in a royal blue dress had her head tilted slightly toward her right shoulder and had pursed lips and a pensive look on her face. As he gazed toward the rear of the auditorium, he spotted a man in a dark suit. He appeared to be about middle aged and his facial expression was serious. Harrison sensed he had seen this man before. He was not enrolled in Harrison's course. Was he auditing the course without Harrison's knowledge?

Harrison finished the lecture and, having answered the questions asked by a few students after class, headed into the hallway and toward his office. He saw the man in the dark suit about thirty feet in front of him. "Sir!" he called out. He wanted to ask the gentleman if he were enjoying the lectures. And he wanted to find out what the man's purpose was in sitting in. But the man turned onto a side corridor and, even though Jonathan reached the turn seconds later, the man was not in sight.

Harrison shrugged and returned to his office. The student in the royal blue dress was waiting there at the door. "Hello, Dr. Harrison, I'm Amy Mitchell," she began. "Yes, of course," Harrison replied as he motioned her into the office. The office was a twelve-foot by fourteen-foot room with light blue walls and a steel-grey carpet. On each of the four walls were two eighteen-by-twenty-four-inch, framed pictures. There were two mountain scenes, two ocean scenes, two astronomy photographs (one of the Andromeda Galaxy and one of Jupiter), a portrait of Albert Einstein, and a portrait of Laozi, the father of Taoism, with the quotation, "Think lightly of yourself and deeply of the world."

Amy sat in the chair at the side of Harrison's desk and waited for her professor to walk to his chair behind the desk and sit. "Professor," she began, "I can't help but notice something. You've taught us about lots of civilizations, and you've described their accomplishments and their failings. You do tell us about their attainments and their greatness, but I can't help but sense more passion in you when you're describing human failings than when you're describing achievements."

Harrison involuntarily raised his right hand to his lips, partially covering his mouth. Then he dropped his hand. His lips were parted and his eyes were unfocused for a moment. Amy looked startled and quickly said, "I'm sorry, Professor, I shouldn't have said anything."

"No, no," said Harrison, "It's okay, really. That's something I need to hear." He paused, and added, "I guess I have to strive for better balance."

Amy took a deep breath, let it out and pursed her lips. "I have the same problem, Professor. I'm an anthropology major. I'm really fascinated by the Mayan civilization. The Maya were great astronomers, architects and mathematicians. But they practiced human sacrifice, and they were warlike. How do you admire the good and ignore the bad, Professor?"

"I'm not sure, Amy. I guess we just have to convince ourselves that increased knowledge will beget enhanced humanity." Allan stroked his chin and looked down. When he looked up, Amy was rising and pulling on her jacket. She spoke, "Thank you, Professor. May I speak with you again?"

Allan replied, "You know my office hours, Amy. Come in any time. And I do welcome your feedback."

———————

Jonathan thought about Amy's comments on his drive home. He involuntarily gritted is teeth as he considered his attitude. Yes, he had idealistic ideas about what humankind could be. Yes, he had reason to be frustrated about the state of human civilization. Yes, his ideas had merit. But no! He did not have the right to try to influence his students to have a similar attitude! Or, did he? If no one spoke out and raised the upcoming generation's awareness of the great discrepancy between what human civilization is and what it could potentially be, then from where would the motivation and creativity come to improve the world? He sighed deeply and shook his head.

Jonathan and Rita had just finished dinner and were sipping some Darjeeling tea. Jonathan appeared distracted, and Rita asked, "Something on your mind, Hon?"

"Yeah!" He replied, "One of my students made a comment to me today after class. She said when I describe civilizations, I do talk about their achievements, but she senses I have more passion when describing their failings. I don't want to be a curmudgeon! I don't want to be a doom and gloomer!"

"Maybe you just have to remember where we came from, sweetie. We branched off from apes six or seven million years ago. We've only had agriculture for eleven thousand years. We've only had written language for four thousand years. Maybe we deserve a pass."

Jonathan nodded, "True, Baby, but Laozi developed the Tao twenty-four hundred years ago. Twenty-four hundred years ago human beings had a philosophy of peace, and of harmony with nature. It makes me think that since then, our 'pass' expired."

———————

Jonathan looked out over his class. He had just extolled the virtues of the early English settlers of the Massachusetts Bay Colony. He hoped he had sufficiently emphasized their adventurous spirit in seeking out a new land and their fortitude at lasting through harsh conditions. He knew he must turn attention to how the Puritans, having ostensibly left England to avoid religious persecution, had then turned around and had dealt out a religious persecution, in the new world, worse than any they had faced in England.

Could he deal with this subject without seeming to be a totally negative person? Could he explain the topic without appearing to relish in the negative? As he looked out over the faces of his students, he saw the man in the dark suit again. "Who is he?" Jonathan thought "And why does he keep showing up for a few minutes at a time in my class?"

When class was over Harrison saw the man in the dark suit disappearing out the back door. Amy was approaching the lectern, but he wanted to seek out the mysterious visitor. He glanced quickly at Amy, said, "I'll be in my office in a few minutes," and hurried out the back after his visitor. He rushed out into the back corridor, looked right and left, and saw his visitor disappearing around a corner. He walked briskly around the corner, and saw the men's room door closing. He hesitated a moment, then pushed open the door to the men's room and walked in.

His mysterious visitor was standing at the back of the room, near the window, facing Jonathan, as if he were expecting him. The man smiled. Jonathan was about to say something, when the man pointed to the door, which locked at his gesture. Jonathan quickly drew in a breath, his heart beating faster. The man held up his right hand in a peaceful gesture, and said, "Relax. I just want to talk with you."

A few moments passed, and Jonathan finally spoke, his voice a little quivery, "Who are you? And why have you been observing my class?"

"We are very much interested in you, Professor Harrison," began the stranger. And I am going to offer you a unique opportunity. You are a man of great intellect and great passion. You have a passion for the beauty of the Universe and of the Earth. And while you have a passion for the heights that human civilization could have attained, you have an even stronger sense of disappointment, and even loathing, for what your civilization has become."

"My civilization?" queried Jonathan.

"Oh, yes, of course," said the stranger. He reached up to his neck, hooked his two thumbs under the collar of his shirt and, as Jonathan gasped with fear, peeled off his face. Jonathan turned to the door, as if to flee, but the visitor's calming voice stopped him. "It's okay, Professor, really." Jonathan turned back and saw that his visitor's face was quite human-looking, though his skin tone was light blue and his eyes were set a little too wide apart. "My name is Salgon, Professor, and I am from a civilization 10,000 years older than your own. We have technologies you would experience as unfathomable. And, as I said, I am here to give you a unique opportunity. Come."

Salgon made a gesture and, suddenly, they were in a forest.

127

"Wait! Where are we?" asked Jonathan.

"We're in a wooded area, about a mile from your school," answered Salgon. "Come on, over here." Salgon led the way along a path to a place where the foliage was particularly dense. He gestured, and the foliage parted, revealing a clearing, in the center of which was . . . . . a flying saucer?

The saucer-shaped craft appeared to be about thirty feet in diameter and about eight feet in height. It was steel-grey in color and had no discernible markings or insignias. Jonathan stammered, "Is that . . .is that . . . a spaceship?"

"More than that," Salgon answered, "It's a space and time ship. Come on aboard."

Jonathan could not put is thoughts and fears into words. "But . . . what . . ."

"We're going to take a little trip," said Salgon, "After which, if you desire, you may return, with nothing changed." A boarding ramp had descended and, though Jonathan's legs felt like wood, he managed to follow Salgon up the ramp and into the ship.

The inside of the ship was bathed in a soft, blue light. There was a center console that went from floor to ceiling. It appeared to be a giant computer screen, lighting up in rhythmic patterns. There were curved alcoves along the outer wall that looked like deep armchairs. Salgon motioned Jonathan to one of the alcoves and reclined into one himself. From overhead a padded harness descended and held Jonathan firmly in place, reminding him of an amusement park ride. He heard a low hum that rose in pitch until it was a whine, and he was overcome by feelings he could not place. He did not know if he were feeing elated or sad, sick or robust, sleepy or alert.

It was as though all feelings existed simultaneously. He lost all sense of the passage of time, but it felt like an eternity. He may have briefly passed out, and he heard Salgon's voice reassuring him that all was well. The harness retreated into the space above, and Salgon was taking Jonathan by the arm just above the elbow and was helping him to his feet.

"Where are we?" asked Jonathan.

"It's not just where; it's when." replied Salgon. He motioned Jonathan over to what appeared to be a viewing port. They seemed to be hanging in mid-air, over a landscape that included savannah to the left and forest to the right, and a small pond beneath them. The land rose sharply about a quarter-mile straight ahead.

"This is Olduvai Gorge in Tanzania. Look below, Dr. Harrison." Jonathan looked and was startled by what he saw. It was a group of . . . . . what? Man-apes? Ape-men? They walked upright, and appeared to be at least five feet in height. They were quite hairy, and wore no clothes. Six or seven males walked out onto the edge of the savannah and paused, apparently watching the grasslands and sniffing the air. Presently, about two dozen more came out of the forested area and gathered at the pond to drink.

"You were serious about the vessel being a space and time ship. When is this?" Asked Jonathan.

"This is 1.5 million years in your past. The beings you see below us are Homo Habilis, the ancestors of Homo Erectus, which are in turn the ancestors of Homo Ergaster, Homo Neanderthalis and Homo Sapiens. Within a day a burst of cosmic rays will strike the upper atmosphere. It will cause a shower of charged particles that will in turn cause a chance mutation. We have determined that the mutation will alter the brains of eight members of this troupe, who will become the founders of an offshoot of this species.

"The mutated individuals will be the founders of a population that will have the ability to think abstractly and to communicate with more complex language. This will set the stage for collective learning which, as you may know, is the crucial factor that sets your species apart from all others on Earth. Without collective learning there would be no agriculture, no towns or cities, no advanced technology . . . no civilization."

"So, why are we here?" asked Jonathan.

"Dr. Harrison," Salgon began, nodding thoughtfully, "You are a severe critic of your civilization. You rail out against man's inhumanity to man and the immense suffering people have inflicted on others. Specifically, you decry cruelty, violence, corruption, slavery, sexual violence, war, and genocide. Those are all products of civilization. They are all, ultimately, among the products of collective learning. You can stop all that."

"There is a button three feet to your right. If you press it, a shield will protect the troupe below from the shower of particles that will be descending. There will be no mutation. There will be no increased ability to think abstractly and to communicate complex ideas. There will be no collective learning and no civilization. There will be no cruelty, violence, corruption, slavery, sexual violence, war, and genocide. Oh, there will be predation. Lions will kill zebras, cheetahs will kill gazelles, and pythons will kill anything they can wrap their coils around. But there will be no systematic subjugation of whole populations by other populations. There will be no burning of coal, oil or methane. There will be no wholesale degradation of coral reefs. The world will remain pristine, just as you have imagined it might have remained had human civilization not interfered."

Jonathan's mouth was open, and his breathing was somewhat shallow and rapid. Finally, he replied," But then Laozi will never develop Taoism. Lippershey will not invent the telescope and Galileo will never discover the moons of Jupiter. Da Vinci will not paint the Mona Lisa, Beethoven will never write a symphony and Einstein will never teach us the nature of gravitation. We won't be here to discover how the Universe began, how stars created elements and how life on Earth originated."

"That is all sadly true, Professor. You have a decision to make. We can go back without your pressing the button. Humankind will have accomplished all that you just mentioned, and more. But along with that you will have to accept the rapes, murders, enslavements, wars, and all the other horrors and suffering you deplore. Press the button, and all humankind's accomplishments will never have existed, and neither will the horrors and suffering. I am going into the other compartment to meditate, Professor. Think it over and make your decision."

"Hold on!" Jonathan looked up sharply. "Why don't you push the button yourself? Why do you need me?"

Salgon shook his head. "It would be unthinkable, and absolutely beneath our ethics. If it were done, it would be done by a member of your civilization. And, it cannot be just any member, but one who cares about your world."

"We could find fifty million malcontents who are miserably unhappy, who have just experienced a major rejection or setback, and who would be glad to impulsively end your world out of frustration. No, no! If your civilization is to be erased, the decision must be made by someone like yourself who has knowledge and perspective. I'm sure it seems extremely strange, but that's the way it is."

"What about me, and my girlfriend Rita?"

Salgon replied, "You will never feel a thing. It will be as though you had suddenly fallen asleep. You will never have existed." Salgon disappeared into another chamber.

Professor Jonathan Harrison moved to the button to which Salgon had directed him. He placed his hand on it. His mind was flooded with images of abduction and slavery, of the horrors of war, of the rape rooms of Saddam Hussein, and of the concentration camps of Hitler. He tried to imagine the feelings of pain, humiliation and utter despair that human beings have experienced at the hands of others. All the horrors and suffering human beings had ever inflicted on one another need not have happened. But neither would the knowledge and accomplishments. His breathing was shallow and his head throbbed. He fell back in his seat with his head lowered and his hands in his lap. He had a decision to make.

Science Fiction Versus Space Opera

Science fiction is a genre of fiction that seeks to tell a story in the context of real or projected scientific and/or technological development. Typically abbreviated sci-fi, science fiction often starts with our current state of technology and science. It then projects imagined advances, and explores their impact on society or individuals. Writers in the past, such as Jules Verne, sometimes dealt with themes common to modern sci-fi. But in telling their stories they did not attempt to be scientifically or technologically plausible.

Even with the supposed restrictions of scientific plausibility, science fiction writers can tell some fascinating tales. Indeed, the very fact of the scientific plausibility can render their stories even more impactful, as we can imagine their actual occurrence in our future.

Space opera is a different, more-fanciful genre, related to sci fi. But creators of space opera, instead of being tied to scientific or technological plausibility, free themselves from those restrictions. They make more frequent use, than do science fiction writers, of devices such as faster-than-light travel, wormholes, and time travel. Space opera creations are typically action adventures, often on a galactic scale. Some of the best-known examples are the Star Trek television shows and movies, and the Star Wars film saga. They portray extremely advanced technology, but also spectacularly fanciful events and situations such as beings with super powers, galactic scale struggles, parallel universes, and English-speaking extra-terrestrials.

There is no clear dividing line between science fiction and space opera. Though space opera typically offers more glitz, readers should not dismiss science fiction as drab, uninteresting or uninspiring in comparison. Sci-fi's intrigue and excitement may include epic journeys, imaginary worlds, utopian aspirations, and prophetic warnings, all usually within, or at least near, the boundaries of credibility.

About the Author

Michael Slavit is a psychologist in private practice. He received his Doctorate in Counseling Psychology at the University of Texas at Austin. Though board certified in Behavioral and Cognitive Psychology by the American Board of Professional Psychology, he considers his most important credential to be the confidence of his patients.

Dr. Slavit has been an avid follower of astronomy for many decades. He has pursued other interests in the sciences, including Earth science and origins of life research, among others.

Dr. Slavit has a variety of writing interests. He is the author of:

- **Embracing fitness**
- **Train Your Wandering Mind: Coping with ADHD**
- **Lessons from Desiderata**
- **Your Life: An Owner's Guide**
- **Cure Your Money Ills: Improve Your Self-esteem through Personal Budgeting**

He has works in process, including

- **U.S. History Through a Prism**
- **A Brief History of the Universe, the Earth and Life**
  (illustrated with limericks)
- **220 Limericks**

Dr. Slavit is intrigued by how far and fast human civilization has come in the development of science and technology. However, as evidenced by his story *The Five Es*, he sees a gap between our science and technology on the one hand, and our human relations ability on the other.

In another of his works, Dr. Slavit writes

As a species we have rocketed forward at super speed in developing our science and our technology. But we have lagged so, so far behind in learning to plan for our future, to set common goals, resolve our differences, envision a common destiny and uplift one another.

Dr. Slavit hopes that his stories are enjoyable and intriguing, but realizes that some may be disquieting as well. He believes that being able to envision less desirable, as well as more desirable, futures is important if people are to be motivated to influence society in positive ways, and if human civilization is to make favorable choices.